### "I've seen it too many times before."

"The innocent look, huh?" he asked. "Who's been overusing it for your benefit lately?"

"Any number of students, especially boys, who think they can put something over on me."

Her merriment was lovely, but it felt fragile, and Mikal wondered why. "Have there been *men* who've thought they could put something over on you?" It occurred to him suddenly that he needed to know.

She looked into his eyes, frankly assessing him. "Not lately," she told him quietly.

"But once upon a time?"

She glanced away. "One...once."

"And now?" She looked back at him, questioning his boldness, and he leaned toward her, bolder still. "Is there anyone now, Morgan?"

His directness prompted hers. "No, there isn't."

"Good." He smiled and settled back in his chair. "That's good."

Dear Reader,

Sophisticated but sensitive, savvy yet unabashedly sentimental—that's today's woman, today's romance reader—you! And Silhouette Special Editions are written expressly to reward your quest for substantial, emotionally involving love stories.

So take a leisurely stroll under the cover's lavender arch into a garden of romantic delights. Pick and choose among titles if you must—we hope you'll soon equate all six Special Editions each month with consistently gratifying romantic reading.

Watch for sparkling new stories from your Silhouette favorites—Nora Roberts, Tracy Sinclair, Ginna Gray, Lindsay McKenna, Curtiss Ann Matlock, among others—along with some exciting newcomers to Silhouette, such as Karen Keast and Patricia Coughlin. Be on the lookout, too, for the new Silhouette Classics, a distinctive collection of bestselling Special Editions and Silhouette Intimate Moments now brought back to the stands—two each month—by popular demand.

On behalf of all the authors and editors of Special Editions,
Warmest wishes,

Leslie Kazanjian
Senior Editor

# KATHLEEN EAGLE
## Candles in the Night

*Silhouette Special Edition*

Published by Silhouette Books New York

**America's Publisher of Contemporary Romance**

For David,
my firstborn

**SILHOUETTE BOOKS**
300 East 42nd St., New York, N.Y. 10017

Copyright © 1988 by Kathleen Eagle

ISBN: 0-373-09437-X

First Silhouette Books printing February 1988

America's Publisher of Contemporary Romance

Printed in the U.S.A.

# KATHLEEN EAGLE

is a transplant to her favorite regional setting, the Dakota prairie. As educator, wife, mother and writer, she believes that a woman's place is wherever she's needed—and anywhere she needs to be.

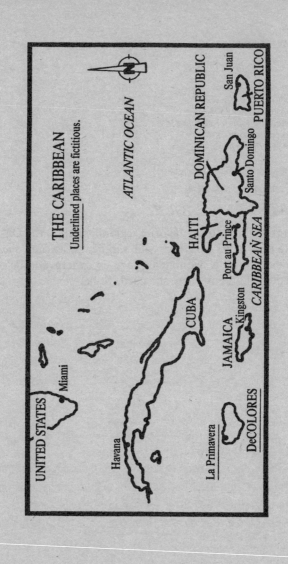

THE CARIBBEAN
Underlined places are fictitious.

UNITED STATES

Miami

Havana

CUBA

JAMAICA

Kingston

La Primavera

DeCOLORES

CARIBBEAN SEA

HAITI

Port au Prince

DOMINICAN REPUBLIC

Santo Domingo

San Juan

PUERTO RICO

ATLANTIC OCEAN

N

## Chapter One

Mikal Romanov reminded himself that he was a patient man as he studied the pictures in Miss Kramer's outer office. There was a watercolor of a prairie schoolhouse, a print of Ben Franklin's portrait, a framed copy of the Declaration of Independence, and John Donne's "No Man is an Island" quotation in decorative calligraphy. Heady stuff, he thought. Franklin and Donne were admirable men, and patient, too, no doubt.

Miss Kramer was on the phone, or so the secretary had told him. She'd be with him in just a moment. He glanced at his watch. That had been ten minutes ago. He'd give the lady another five. His patience notwithstanding, he'd never enjoyed sitting in the principal's office.

Studying the knowing look in Ben Franklin's piercing eyes, Mikal absently drew a quarter from his pocket and flipped it with his thumb. On the third flip, the coin escaped him, rolling under a chair near the inner office's closed door. Mikal squatted and reached for the quarter just as the office door opened. He hesitated, turned his head and encountered first a pair of black pumps, then sleek ankles, and finally two very silky, sexy legs. They were such great legs that he had no desire to lift his eyes any higher.

"Mr. Romanov?"

Mikal glanced up quickly. Her eyes were cold, but her face matched her legs—unmistakably feminine. He smiled. "How do you do, Miss Kramer? I thought it would be simplest just to cower right from the start."

"I see." The smile she returned was patient. "You were expecting the worst?"

"Much worse." He dared another glance at her legs as he uncoiled his own, rising slowly to tower above her. "But not *the* worst. The worst was Mr. Pross, the principal who saw to it that I was benched on a regular basis."

"Did you turn the lab mice loose, too?"

"No. My son can take credit for thinking that one up on his own." She was the epitome of primness. She looked as if she needed a wicked grin, so he gave her one. "But I did sell tickets to the peephole into the girls' locker room. I paid for the damages on that one, too."

"Somehow I think those damages might have been irreparable." She lifted an admonishing eyebrow. "Please come into my office, Mr. Romanov."

Her voice, low and dignified, carried such foreboding that he hastened to explain. "We couldn't really see much. It was just the idea."

"Sit down, Mr. Romanov," she instructed, again with the patience of someone accustomed to being the only adult in the room. He watched her move crisply around her desk and sit down. Her dark hair was pinned neatly at the back of her head. She wore a charcoal-gray tailored suit, and the only hint of frivolity Mikal detected in her outfit was the small ruffle on the high collar of her wine-colored blouse. The ruffle dipped when she lowered her chin to look at some papers on her desk—papers that undoubtedly recounted David's education from birth through the eighth grade. Another narrow ruffle framed her wrist as she turned a page. She wore no jewelry, no nail polish, and her nails were sensibly trimmed. Only the small bit of burgundy ruffle was there to accent the softness of her slight hand. She was lovely, but she was probably one of the few women who preferred to be considered attractive or distinguished. "Attractive" fell short of describing her, and Mikal figured she was about thirty years too young for "distinguished."

Morgan folded her hands on top of the pile of papers—which had nothing to do with David Romanov. She took a long, slow breath before looking across the desk at the man who had, surprisingly, seated himself in the place she'd indicated. She'd expected him to take another chair or to stand in the doorway—anything but what she'd suggested. She knew how rebels behaved.

"The mice are not the reason I've requested this meeting," Morgan began, lifting her chin first, then her eyes. "David will be required to pay for them, and for the cost of exterminating them."

Mikal winced, squirming as his son had surely done when he'd been sitting in the same chair. "The mice had to be exterminated?"

She dipped her chin in solemn confirmation. "One of them turned up in the home economics lab. The teacher was certain we had an infestation, and we do have health codes to consider. I've explained to David that he must bear those expenses, and I hope you won't bail him out on that. It should be his responsibility."

"I realize that." She was lovely, yes, but he was beginning to chafe a little. Didn't she think he knew how to raise his own kid?

"Good. The real problem here, Mr. Romanov, is the recent decline in David's academic efforts. Several of his teachers have reported a marked change in attitude. He hasn't been doing his assignments. Report cards will be out soon, and I'm afraid David's grades won't be as good as they have been in the past."

Morgan watched the effect the news had on Mikal Romanov's face. His brow furrowed, and he fixed his eyes on hers. "What kind of change in attitude? He's not giving his teachers any trouble, is he?"

"David is never rude, of course. He's a very pleasant boy—personable and well-mannered." That assurance brought relief and then, predictably, satisfaction to the father's face. "He's simply not doing his job here."

Mikal shook his head slowly. "I guess I've eased up on him lately. I've been leaving it up to him to get his homework done. I'll get back on his case."

"Mr. Romanov, your son is very bright. He's been in the gifted and talented program, and his teachers know his potential. We try very hard to—"

"Yes, I know. You try hard; I try hard; and David works like hell when it catches his fancy." Mikal offered an apologetic smile and an open-handed gesture. He'd fought this battle over his son before. "He doesn't always respond to traditional methods of teaching."

"We're aware of that," Morgan assured him, laying her palms carefully on the papers in front of her. "But no matter how talented an individual may be, there are certain responsibilities we all have, certain mundane tasks we all must perform every day. Chores, paperwork, schedules—we all learn to deal with those things or we go down in the mire of our own disorganization."

His laughter caught her off guard, and she gave him a wide-eyed stare. "Now you're talking about David's old man," Mikal confessed, shifting in his chair.

"We start talking organization, and *he's* the one who gets on *my* case."

"I see." Morgan folded her hands and studied the even row of her knuckles. She saw a great deal, and that made it difficult to keep a steady eye on the man. He was casually dressed in a yellow sweater vest, and a brown corduroy sports jacket, with corduroy pants, and he looked completely comfortable. His tawny hair curled around his ears and tumbled over his forehead in a style that probably required only the use of his fingers as a comb. He smiled easily, laughed even more easily, and his clear blue eyes invited her to laugh with him—even *at* him, if she'd succumb to the temptation. But she wouldn't. He was undoubtedly as charming as he was handsome, but concern for a student's well-being was not a matter to be charmed away. "David may fail English this quarter."

Mikal laughed again, and this time Morgan frowned at him. He dismissed the threat with a wave of his hand. "David reads as much as I do. His writing may be a little undisciplined, but he's only thirteen. He's creative; what more can you ask?"

"He isn't doing his work, Mr. Romanov. His vocabulary assignments—"

"He has an excellent vocabulary." This point was couched in a less jovial tone.

"I realize that, but he is not doing his vocabulary *assignments*. He may be a creative writer, but he isn't writing. We cannot evaluate what we cannot see."

Mikal's hands went up in surrender. "Okay. You're right. No excuses. We'll talk this over and get it straightened out. I didn't realize he'd slacked off this much. Maybe I haven't spent enough time with him lately.''

Guilt. Morgan had seen a lot of it in her work, and she knew it weighed heavily on parents. Her job wasn't easy, but she imagined that being a father was much harder, especially for a single man. She remembered David's bid for sympathy when she'd had him in her office. ''I don't have a mother, Miss Kramer. He's all I've got, and we've gotten to the point where we don't even speak the same language. He's literally not of this world.''

''Not of this world'' was probably putting it mildly. From what she'd heard, the man had his head in the clouds. All for a good cause, of course. Morgan smiled, remembering her middleman's role. ''Your son is very proud of you. In fact, I think he feels you're a bit larger than life, and he's afraid he can't measure up.''

He was surprised by her statement, as well as by her smile, which was warming up a little. ''Measure up to what? The work I do best doesn't pay, and I can't find much time for what I do second best—which pays only when I do it.'' Mikal lifted a shoulder and smiled again. ''*That's* lack of organization, Miss Kramer. David sees me in my natural state, and it isn't larger than life, believe me.''

There was something admirable in his honest admission, and Morgan caught his eye in a frank exchange. He wasn't a saint. Neither was he a great sinner. He was a man, concerned about his son and willing to tell Morgan the long and the short of his existence in order to clarify the situation. David's father was just like any other father.

Hardly, she reminded herself. His voice said "believe me" but his eyes were more effective than his words. Their crystal-blue honesty could suck a listener in before the man opened his mouth. And Morgan was not about to forget the kind of man he was. Charming dreamers were her Achilles' heel.

"David lists his father's occupation as 'writer,' but that isn't the real source of your fame," Morgan said, allowing herself, against her better judgment, to show an interest in his activities. "I think...that is, I'm sure the whole *community* shares David's pride in your...your work."

"If you're talking about Freedom International, it's the work of a lot of people, and all of them deserve commendations. I feel a little self-conscious about being singled out."

"They gave you a big write-up in the paper."

"It was a nice honor, but it could have been divided a hundred ways." He shifted again in his chair. The man who had been completely at ease had suddenly become uncomfortable. Morgan noticed that his size overwhelmed the small chair she had given him. If she could have done it without making him even more self-conscious, she would have offered him a different one.

"But you seem to be an eloquent spokesman, Mr. Romanov. From what I've read, your organization has been instrumental in securing freedom for a number of political prisoners.''

He shrugged. ''We can't always get them out, but we find that sometimes just by drawing attention to them, we can improve conditions.''

''Do you travel much for your work?'' She knew full well that he must, and she wondered how that affected David.

''Some. I also write a lot of letters, draft a lot of petitions.'' He cocked his head to the side and smiled. ''Would you care to sign one? I have two with me— one protesting the proposed new missile base and the other...'' He laid a hand over one side of his jacket, but his smile said that he knew better than to reach inside.

''Another time, maybe. My concern right now is for David's attitude and what influences may be affecting it adversely.'' Rolling her chair back from the desk, Morgan put more distance between them as she made a gable of her hands, her habitual ''discussion'' gesture, and launched into a personal aside as impersonally as she could manage. ''You see, I believe I understand David's viewpoint even better than you do. My father is a minister—a missionary, in fact. His work is his life, and his ideals are impeccable. It's very difficult for a child—'' eyeing the man quickly, she saw that he was interested ''—*any* child, to assert his own needs when the needs of... of hungry people—'' she risked another glance ''—of people who are imprisoned unjustly, are at stake. Sometimes a child does whatever he thinks is necessary to get his father's attention." She hastened to add, "Unconsciously, of course."

"Are you thinking maybe I'm letting my causes take precedence over my son?"

She didn't answer. Her eyes became a mirror and he saw the reflection of all his worries, all the doubts he'd had since the death of David's mother some ten years ago. "It's for David that I do what I do," he said quietly. "I love my son, and I want to give him a better world."

Morgan glanced away, taking the time to put that beautiful ideal into perspective. She returned to a matter-of-fact approach. "I appreciate that, Mr. Romanov. Someday David will, too. My concern is with giving him a better education, and I think you need to be aware that he hasn't been cooperating with that effort lately."

"I think he's playing a game with both of us, Miss Kramer. I'll find out what it is and see that he stops."

She stood, and he followed suit, watching her move around the desk as she explained, "What seems like a game to us might be serious business for David. Children's minds work in mysterious ways."

As she stepped in front of him, reaching for the door, Mikal noticed the small wisps of hair that fringed the back of her neck, defying the restrictions her severe hairstyle tried to impose on them. They looked soft, and he had a sudden urge to blow on them and make them flutter—just to see if she had a giggle in her. He smiled, believing she might. He suspected

David believed she did, too. David was probably after somebody's attention, all right, but not his dad's.

"I appreciate your taking the time—"

"My time belongs to my students," she said, offering her hand. "I can't let a problem like David's slip by me."

Of that he had no doubt. He took her hand in his and pressed it, palm to palm, in a gesture that in no way suggested a final goodbye. She looked up, and he took stock of the features she couldn't play down—the fine bone structure, the translucent white skin, the brown-green eyes. If David harbored a crush on this woman, it was well-founded, Mikal decided. "I'll call you in a week or so," he promised, "to see if we're making progress."

"Yes," Morgan managed in a voice much smaller than it had been during the entire meeting, "that will be fine."

Morgan closed the door and leaned her back against it. She felt a little weak-kneed because...well, the man *was* charming. Predictably so, she reminded herself, moving toward her desk and sitting down. She pulled a three-day-old copy of the *Tribune* from the bottom drawer. Recent publicity had probably given David's father folk-hero status in some circles across the country, but the people of Bismarck were generally conservative. He'd made the news with a presidential commendation for his work with Freedom International, but the headline was dwarfed by the one announcing a hike in hog prices.

The photograph of Mikal Romanov with two other members of the organization confirmed her idea that he was not obsessed with appearances, but that he exuded a kind of magnetism, something that drew the eye to his face. Handsome, yes, but more than that he was . . . an idealist, Morgan told herself as she leaned back in her chair, putting some distance between herself and the picture. A cockeyed optimist. An aging hippie. The man was zealous in his pursuit of causes— world peace, freedom for political prisoners, affirmative action, clean water. Morgan knew the type. Buoyed up by their own charisma, men like him were completely impractical, totally unpredictable, and produced very little in the way of tangible results.

No wonder David was acting up. At his age he needed less zeal and more stability. He was a very clever young man, but the same battle raged within him as in every thirteen-year-old. He wanted to grow up, but he didn't want to leave childhood behind. Morgan smiled, remembering the boy's wide-eyed expression of innocence when she'd confronted him with the charges against him.

"The fault, Miss Kramer, is not in my stars, but in my father." She'd told him to try that one on his English teacher. "Really," he'd insisted. "The man is driving me crazy. Which explains my insane behavior: Independence Day for the white mice in the science lab."

The boy's dark brown eyes weren't quite as overwhelming as his father's, but then he'd had fewer years to perfect the knack, and already he was hard to resist. She'd explained to him that, though he'd have to pay for the mice, her real concern was for his falling grades, which were not his father's responsibility.

David had agreed, at least in part. "I'm responsible for my grades. He's responsible for my insanity. I've become a madman."

Morgan had noticed the three books he'd set by the chair; science, math, and Salinger's *Catcher in the Rye*. "Just lately?" she'd asked.

"Salinger has nothing to do with this," David had assured her. "He's prehistoric. I'm talking major insanity here. Do you know what it's like to be the son of a saint?"

It was an interesting question. She was the daughter of one, which might be less taxing than the role of a son. She wondered what was expected of a boy whose father had been honored by the president simply for helping people. Her own father's work had received little notice, and he required none. He went right on with his mission even now, when by all rights he should have been spending a comfortable retirement with what family he had left.

"Everybody thinks he's such a great man," David had said. "At least, they say they do, but they're probably thinking he's weird. Great, but weird."

Yes, Morgan thought, for Bismarck, Mikal Romanov was a little different. He would have to move much farther east or west to find an active community of believers. *Dreamers*, Morgan amended. She wondered why he chose to stay among the practical conservatives who were the backbone of central North Dakota.

Morgan glanced at the picture in the paper and then at the small chair in front of her desk. That chair had only made him seem bigger, a circumstance made more charming by the fact that he hadn't complained. His modest squirm when she'd mentioned his award had been a nice touch, too. Despite all that, she'd dealt with the matter just as she'd intended; David would pay for the damages, and his schoolwork would be closely monitored.

Folding the newspaper in half, Morgan eyed the trashcan beside her desk, but she tucked the paper back in the bottom drawer, stopping for one more glimpse of Mikal Romanov's charming smile before she slid the drawer closed.

David stumbled over a pair of size thirteen running shoes when he came home. He wondered why he hadn't expected the shoes to be there since that was where his dad always kept them—just inside the back door, waiting to trip all comers.

That minor annoyance quickly took a backseat to the aromatic promise that filled the kitchen. David moved to the stove, lifted the lid on the steaming kettle and took a deep whiff. Hungarian goulash. The clutter at the back door was forgiven.

"Dad? You home?"

Even in stockinged feet, Mikal Romanov's approach was clearly audible. He never climbed the basement stairs; he bounded up two steps at a time.

The jogging shoes or whatever else he'd left by the door were never in his way. Dressed in gray sweats, he came into the kitchen looking like the professional football player David often wished his father was. He was big enough, David thought as he turned a sheepish grin at Mikal. "Got my nose ground down at the sweatshop today. I'm starved." David inhaled dramatically. "Supper smells great."

Mikal registered the compliment with a grain of salt as he straddled a kitchen chair and folded his arms atop the back. "I got started a little late this afternoon; it'll be a while yet. Hard day, huh?"

David ducked into the refrigerator, took a quick survey and reached for the crisper drawer. "Full of the usual stuff we've done a hundred times. I hope they think of something new for high school." He came up with two apples and, with a questioning look, held one up in Mikal's direction.

"I hope so, too." Mikal gave a nod, and the apple flew through the air and whacked into his big hand. "If they don't, you will."

The refrigerator door swung closed, and David hung his head in a small act of contrition. "It's just what I said, Dad, the mice were like a mountain. They were there, waiting to be—"

"No sale on that one, David. And I think the bill you have to pay will keep you out of circulation for some time."

True, David thought, but the stunt had accomplished one thing. His dad had introduced himself to Miss Kramer. David tried to inject a note of dread into his voice. "So you had your conference with Miss Kramer today, huh?"

"We're concerned about your schoolwork, son."

David joined his father at the table and sank his teeth into the sweet red apple. *We're* concerned. He liked the sound of that. He hoped this meant his dad would be conferring with Miss Kramer on a regular basis. "It's no big deal, Dad. It's probably hormones."

"Hormones?" Mikal felt a smile coming on that he'd just as soon repress.

"Yeah, you know. I'm at that age."

"Girls becoming a distraction, are they?" Not yet, Mikal hoped. He wasn't ready to let his son's boyhood go, and he sent up a silent prayer for one more year of skateboards and vintage comic books.

"Not so much." David hooked his right ankle over his left knee and watched his own foot jiggle. Then a memory made him smile. "But it was pretty funny when that mouse jumped out of Jenny Dutton's purse in science class. You never heard such a shriek."

"Now you have to pay the piper." Mikal's smile was getting away from him as he remembered the day when the news of the locker-room peephole hit the cheerleading squad. "The Pied Piper—he was an exterminator, too, remember? And after supper you hit the books."

David offered a bony-shouldered, adolescent shrug. "No problem, Dad. I was just taking a little mid-semester hiatus. So, uh..." He risked an upward glance. "What'd you think of Miss Kramer?"

Mikal considered. "I guess I thought...for a principal, she wasn't half bad." His eyebrows went up a notch as he added, "Quite fair, in fact. She could have thrown the book at us—at *you*."

"I mean..." David hedged. He didn't want to push too quickly, but he did want to know. "What did you think of...like her looks, for instance."

"'Her looks, for instance,'" Mikal repeated as he bit into his apple. David had very good taste, he thought, remembering the dark wisps of hair against the fine porcelain of her neck. "Fair," he said, adding quietly and with a wistful smile, "Fair and very, very fine."

"I think...I mean the *kids* think...I mean we *all* pretty much like her." David paused to check for reactions. His father was all ears. "She's nice, once you get to know her. Strict, you know, but good sense of humor, and fair, just like you said. And, uh, I don't know if you noticed, but...she's got a really good set of legs."

The bite of apple nearly took a wrong turn in Mikal's throat. Yes, indeed, he had noticed, and he hoped David hadn't been anywhere around when he'd been introducing himself to the lady's hemline. "She probably has nice hair, too," he volunteered, "when it's not done up in that knot."

"Probably. She said she saw your picture in the paper. I think she was kind of impressed."

"You think so?"

"Well, she asked a lot of questions about you."

Mikal swung his leg over the chair and moved to the stove. "She did, huh?" He stuck a spoon in the goulash and stirred slowly. "Hope you didn't tell her any bad stuff."

"What bad stuff? There isn't any."

Mikal ducked his head under a bank of cupboards to look at his son and grinned. "Is that Romanov diplomacy I hear?"

"Maybe a little," David admitted. "I figure it can't hurt."

"Neither can my keeping close tabs on your progress in school."

"You mean..."

Mikal nodded. "I mean I'll be checking in with Miss Kramer." David turned his chair toward the table and planted his chin in his hands. "Regularly. I think that's what's called for now, don't you?" Mikal asked the back of his son's head.

David managed a joyless "I guess I've got it coming" as he directed a slow Cheshire-cat grin at the opposite wall.

## Chapter Two

David Romanov had given hours of thought to his prospects for family life in the immediate future, and he decided that his father's meeting with Miss Kramer had improved the outlook enormously. The dinner conversation that night more than once centered on Mikal's interest in her, and David worked her name in several times to test the waters further. His father took the bait each time. The interest was there, and David liked that idea. In fact, the more he thought about it, the better he liked it. He had only vague memories of his mother and absolutely no reservations about having his father bring another woman into the family. While Mikal dreamed of peace in his time, David dreamed of order, the kind he hoped might arrive with a woman around the house.

Figuring in his head, David concluded that Miss Kramer ought to be perfect for his father. For one thing, she made a very nice living, and although Mikal Romanov was a good man, making a lot of money was not one of the things he was good at. If the Romanovs were to have a serious breadwinner, David's father would have to marry one. Miss Kramer was efficient, ambitious and actually pretty cool for an adult. Her looks were nothing to complain about, either. In David's mind it all added up to a good prospect, one he intended to encourage. He excused himself from the table and went to his room, where dreams and schemes had a way of taking shape. He rummaged through his gym bag.

Getting a romance going required dates—at least, for the "older generation" it did. As always, his father was busy. There was a fund-raiser coming up in Philadelphia, from which Mikal had asked to be excused. He was a grass roots man, he said. He was working on a local rally and trying to write another book. But the executive board of Freedom International knew what it had in Mikal Romanov, and the members wanted his charm to work its magic in Philadelphia. He'd grumble about it, but in another couple of weeks he'd decide to go, so there wasn't much time. David sorted through a handful of printed tickets with a calculating smile on his face. His father didn't have time right now to arrange a date with Miss Kramer. David did.

\* \* \*

The auditorium was filling up fast. It buzzed with the excitement of the friends and relatives of the children who were about to perform. Morgan scanned the crowd as she stepped down from the stage. The parents stood out from the rest, their eyes bright with anticipation, a contrast to the stage fright Morgan had just seen in the students backstage. She'd told them to break a leg, drawing a terrible groan from Jason Rikhert, whose part called for some acrobatics.

Morgan greeted adults and children by name as she made her way toward her seat. David Romanov had sold her a ticket for "the best seat in the house." Ten-A, she reminded herself, scanning the auditorium. There it was, and there was David's father, occupying what was probably the second-best seat in the house. Morgan found herself needing a moment before taking the seat next to him with a collected "How nice to see you again, Mr. Romanov."

His grandmother's old-world training brought him to his feet quickly, and he smiled. "Miss Kramer. Is this your seat?" She nodded in response to his gesture, and since hers was to the inside, he stepped in front of it and offered his. "I'm told *this* is the best seat in the house. Be my guest."

She returned a smile, and her cheeks grew warm. "I think we bought our tickets from the same salesman."

"I have no doubt of it. What other kid would seat his father next to the school principal after he'd set the lab mice loose just the week before?"

"Just David." As she sat, Morgan smoothed her skirt with one hand, waving any concern away with the other. "But that's all taken care of, and tonight is David's night. I understand he's quite the actor."

The truth dawned slowly, but Mikal couldn't miss it when it finally arrived. David had something up his sleeve. Mikal nodded, grinning. "Much better than I'd realized."

"I usually get a chance to peek in on the dress rehearsal, but I missed it this time." The house lights dimmed. Both of them made a point of looking toward the stage, but each took a turn at glancing furtively at the other as the performance got under way.

The play was a spoof of an old melodrama, and David was delightfully nefarious as the villain. Despite her egalitarian attitude toward her students, she found herself concentrating on the boy whose father's presence in the seat next to her was almost overpowering. As she watched David, Mikal's rich laughter found favor in her ears, and his eyes, when they caught hers, blazed with warmth.

The warmth was easily explained. It was his pride in his son, Morgan told herself. He glanced at her occasionally—just to see if she caught each subtle nuance in David's performance, she was sure. They were harmless glances—the kind that would only make her uncomfortable if she allowed them to. The tingling she felt inside must be imaginary.

"You're allowed to laugh out loud, Miss Kramer." Morgan turned to find Mikal leaning close to her. He glanced down at the hands clasped in her lap. "You look like you're having a little sympathetic stage fright," he whispered.

"I probably am." She returned his smile, telling herself that must be it. These were her kids.

"Do I make you nervous?" She gave him a questioning look, and he shrugged. "Just a hunch."

Morgan tried to remember what was going on up front as she made every effort to dismiss his comment. It didn't work. "Why would you think you—"

"Because you make me nervous," he whispered. He was looking at the stage, but his attention was clearly on her.

"I won't keep you after school," she promised. A "shush" from behind brought hot color to Morgan's face, and she heard Mikal's laughter above the rest. She'd missed another gag line. Yes, he definitely made her nervous.

"Join us for an ice-cream cone after the show," Mikal suggested close to her ear. "Ice cream's great for the nerves."

Absurd as that notion was, Morgan found herself agreeing to the invitation. David, on the other hand, declined. After the show was over and the accolades were handed around, he explained quickly that his friend Scott had invited several of the boys to his house for pizza. It was with a sense of great personal satisfaction that David watched his father leave the auditorium with Miss Kramer.

"This changes our options. Do you really want ice cream, or would you rather have a drink?"

Morgan's answer came after Mikal had flicked the rock and roll music off and the heater on. "Ice cream's fine."

"There'll probably be fifty chattering teenagers in every booth, along with video game sound effects and heavy-metal background music."

True. It was Friday night, and she'd earned a respite. "A drink, then."

"Have your cake and eat it, too." He flashed her a smile in passing as he directed his attention to the rearview mirror. "An ice-cream drink."

"Mmm. I'll take all three—the drink, the ice cream *and* the cake. I missed dessert tonight." He had switched from reverse to low gear and was pulling out of the parking lot when the engine made an unmistakable thunk. "Sounds like you're in for some transmission trouble," Morgan remarked.

"Wouldn't surprise me. I had radiator trouble last month. I've got over a hundred thousand miles on this old bomb." He patted the dash. "She's served gallantly."

In the dark, Morgan raised an appreciative brow. Every mile showed. "Maybe it's time for a trade-in."

"You're kidding. Nobody wants her but me."

"You're very tolerant." She'd expected flamboyant. He was a writer and an activist, a combination she would have thought would add up to his having a car with more flash, and probably another date for tonight, as well. "And . . . conservative, maybe?"

"Conservative!" His laughter was unreserved, rolling freely from his chest. "There's a truly insulting epithet. A lady shouldn't use such language."

"I didn't mean politically. I meant economically. Obviously you're not much of a consumer."

"The economy seems to take its course without my wholehearted participation. I think someone else has been assigned to consume my share." As he took a corner, he glanced her way. Her hair was done up neatly in a bun, and there was a heady scent of expensive perfume in the air. A diamond stud flashed in her ear as they passed under a streetlight. "Was it you?"

"I doubt it," she returned, eyeing him cautiously.

"Too bad. I was hoping it was a sensible, hardworking woman who deserved a few creature comforts and a bauble or two." Shifting into second gear, he slowed the car for a turn. "Probably some oil tycoon."

"Probably." She figured Mikal could have his share if he wanted it. In the time since he'd come to her office, she'd made a point of reading his last book. It was a collection of vignettes that were pulled together to form a powerful picture of rural life. It told of the second and third generations of immigrants to the Dakota farmlands whose road was not marked as clearly as their parents' and whose journey had become stagnant. The book had been the basis for a film, a piece that made a statement and won awards but was not a box-office hit. Mikal Romanov was clearly talented enough to write whatever he chose to. He hadn't chosen the best-seller market, or any mar-

ket for that matter, for the last five years. Morgan
wondered why.

The night spot Mikal chose was quiet, far removed
from the idea of fifty teenagers per booth and blaring
music. The decor consisted of rural-looking antiques,
and the music was Viennese strings. They sat across
from one another at a corner table, and the drinks they
ordered were a small price to pay for the privilege of
occupying such a comfortable corner of the world for
a while.

"I read *The Last Barnraising*," Morgan announced. "I thought it was beautiful. I don't know
why I hadn't read it before."

Mikal's eyes danced knowingly, a flicker of candlelight caught in them. "Probably because you're not a
country girl anymore, or you don't want to think of
yourself as one."

"I don't think I've ever thought of myself as a
country girl. My family traveled a great deal when I
was a child."

She'd said her father was a missionary. What she
hadn't said was why she had trouble parting with that
information. He remembered the way she'd glanced
down at her hands and carefully enunciated the word
"missionary" as though she were testing out a foreign phrase. He leaned forward, elbows on the table,
arms forming a tepee over his glass. "Where did you
live?"

"Everywhere that was nowhere," she said lightly.
"Places that were beautiful and barren. Africa, Cen-

tral America, South America. Places that draw few tourists."

"How old were you?"

"I was twelve when my mother decided it was time to come home. Until that point the missionary life was all I knew." She remembered the heat very well, remembered it especially well on cold winter days. A few minutes in a sauna brought back the humidity, but she missed the smell of damp earth and thick vegetation. "North Dakota was my mother's home. After she and I came back here, we saw much less of my father."

"He continued with his work?"

"He had to," she told him. "My father *is* his work. He used to come home more often when my mother was alive, but now..." Morgan's shrug indicated a dismissal of regret. "I think he's somewhere in the Caribbean at the moment."

Mikal nodded thoughtfully. He knew how such a thing might happen, and it wasn't what he wanted for himself. Work should be an extension of the man, not the man himself. In the shadowy candlelight he saw Morgan's regret, heard it in her voice, and it occurred to him that she cared more about her father than she was willing to admit. "You had a fantastic education, then, as the daughter of a missionary. You saw the world as most people never see it."

"Yes, I did." Most of all, she remembered the children. She remembered feeling akin to them but never really one of them. Sometimes she'd wished her father could see her as one of the suffering, because he worked so feverishly to serve them. "We have so much," he would say, "and they have so little." It made her feel guilty to envy them anything, but she did. They had her father's heart. She would never reclaim it, because he would never retire from his work. "Does your kind of work take you out of the country very often?" Morgan wondered.

Mikal shook his head as he raised his glass, sipping from it before he answered. "I have an uncle who's very much involved at the international level, and he's included me on a couple of missions. I'd rather work locally, try to get people involved. Once or twice a year I help out with a fund-raiser. I know how to charm the bucks out of people's billfolds." He gave her a smile and a look that she was sure often did the job before he opened his mouth to speak.

"I see. Does this mean the drinks might be on me?"

Mikal laughed. "Absolutely not. My grandmother would turn over in her grave." He raised a forefinger. "But I warn you, if you come to a rally, you're fair game."

"Forewarned is forearmed." He could think again. She'd been fair game for the likes of him once, and she'd learned her lesson. "Romanov is Russian. Are you related to royalty?"

"Distantly, I guess. My grandparents escaped the Bolsheviks in 1917 with my uncle Yuri, the one I told you about. He was just a young child. An older brother was arrested, and no one knows what happened to him. If he were alive, he'd be in his eighties now. My dad was born in this country, here in North Dakota. My grandfather became a farmer, and my father after him. But my uncle Yuri became an agitator." Mikal's smile indicated the direction of his own sympathies. "An irritant in the world's craw, he calls himself. He was never able to find out what happened to his brother, but he helped found Freedom International. When the organization won the Nobel Peace Prize, it was my uncle Yuri who was there to accept the check."

"Did he put it to good use?"

Mikal's eyes flashed. "Freedom International puts every penny it gets to good use. Would you like a rundown?"

"I'll take your word for it," Morgan offered quickly. "I know a good social conscience when I see one."

"Because you grew up with one?"

She nodded. "How does David feel about all this?"

At the sound of his son's name, Mikal's eyes brightened, again, but his brilliant, "public" smile grew softly private. "David thinks his old man's a little crazy, but he loves me just the same. I think he's going to be a computer whiz or a physicist or something. Analytical, practical and organized—that's David."

"Do those things clash with your dreams for him?"

"My dream for him is peace of mind," Mikal explained, his shrug adding that that went without saying. "I want him to be comfortable with himself and to respect the rest of us." Smiling, he used a finger to punctuate. "Including the mice in the lab and the girls in the locker room."

"Bravo. On behalf of mice and girls alike, I thank you." Mikal dipped his head in acknowledgement. Morgan's smile faded as she let her gaze drop back to her glass. "Aren't you afraid a physicist might lose sight of the ideals you've instilled if he's offered a hundred thousand dollars a year to invent better bombs?" It gave her a perverse pleasure to play the devil's advocate, and she had no idea why.

"Not David," Mikal said, no doubts in his mind. "He'll be his own man. I think I've given him that much."

Morgan nodded, but she was thinking that she was her own woman and no one had given her that. She had claimed it for herself, and she was certainly comfortable with herself. She felt a degree of kinship with David. "He's definitely an individual. I enjoy having him in my phys ed group."

Mikal's frown was an expression of his interest. "You teach a physical education class? I'd have taken you for a former social studies teacher."

"I am." Morgan smiled. How had she given herself away? It pleased her that he'd studied her closely enough to come to that conclusion. "I also teach aerobics, which is what David elected to take this quarter."

"Aerobics? I thought he'd signed up for soccer."

"That was last quarter. We just switched."

As he leaned back in his chair, Mikal digested this news as carefully as he did any foreign dish. Aerobics? David? "How's the gender ratio in aerobics class?"

"Heavy on the females, but that doesn't seem to bother David."

Mikal's slow grin indicated that he thought his son was a chip off the old block. "Wouldn't bother me, either. How do you have time to teach a phys ed class?"

"I think every principal should stay in touch with teaching. I taught a world history class until I had to give the phys ed teacher another chance at driver's ed, so I took up the slack in the gym. I'm saving myself an hour in the evening by doing my exercise during the day."

Mikal leaned forward again, concentrating on her eyes. They came to life in the candlelight. She was telling him about something she obviously considered to be one of her few self-indulgences, and she'd begun to apologize. "What do you do with that extra hour in the evening?" he asked, his voice smooth.

"I go to exercise class anyway, but at least I don't feel obligated." She gathered her nerve. "I enjoy working out."

"Why shouldn't you?"

She shrugged, and his eyes were drawn to the knot of hair at her neck. It was beginning to feather away from its anchor at the back of her head and the wispy tendrils at her temples were all the more attractive because they hadn't been styled. "I didn't used to. I started exercising because I was sitting at a desk too much. I had to push myself at first, but one night when I was shaving my legs in the shower at the Y, I found this terrible lump in my leg." His frown deepened, but she dismissed it quickly. "Right in the back of my thigh. I discovered it was a muscle. I couldn't believe it."

Mikal laughed easily, and Morgan joined him. "I wonder if they have a peephole over there. I'd love to have seen the expression on your face." When she pursed her lips in mock scolding, he added, "That's all I would have looked at—the expression on your face. I swear!"

"Nice try, Mikal, but the innocent look doesn't fool me for a minute." She was smiling again, enjoying the feeling that she had charm to return. "I've seen it too many times before."

He liked the sound of his name as it came from her throat, the *k* catching crisply on the back of her tongue. She was trying it out, testing the sound of it, deciding whether it was a name she wanted to say often. "The innocent look, huh?" he protested. "Who's been overusing it for your benefit lately?"

"Any number of boys who think they can put something over on me."

Her merriment was lovely, but it felt fragile, and Mikal wondered why. When he wondered, it was his habit to be gentle, to ask his questions in a soft voice. "Have there been men who've thought they could put something over on you?" It occurred to him suddenly that he needed to know.

She looked into his eyes, frankly assessing him. What was the source of the gentleness in his voice? Where did the softness in his eyes come from? "Not lately," she told him quietly.

"But once upon a time?"

She glanced away. "One . . . once."

"And now?" She looked back at him, questioning his boldness, and he leaned toward her, bolder still. "Is there anyone now, Morgan?"

His directness prompted hers. "No, there isn't."

"Good." He smiled and settled back in his chair. "That's good."

Morgan turned the name over and over in her mind as she prepared for bed that night. Mikal Romanov. It was a beautiful name, a fairy-tale name. It somehow matched the rich shade of blue in his eyes, a shade that ranged in texture from that of gemstones to soft velvet. Royal blue, sky blue—lofty and vast. She knew better than to let that shade lure her feet to leave the ground. It was not her color. It was a dreamy color— dancer, dramatist, dreamer's delight. Dreamers, all dreamers, should come with warning labels, she decided. Caution: Hard to Resist and Impossible to Guarantee.

She studied herself in the mirror, looking for symptoms of an overdose. She'd been down this road before. Twice in fact. Her father was a dreamer, just like this man. And Jeremy, that impossible, impractical artist she'd actually considered marrying when she was young and foolish—he was a dreamer, too. Fortunately she'd had the sense—well, *he'd* taken the initiative, but she'd had the sense to agree that it would never have worked. Don't fall in love with a dreamer, Morgan. She gave herself a hard stare and said the words aloud so that she could hear them and heed them. "*Don't* fall in love with a dreamer, Morgan."

"So, Dad, how was Miss Kramer?"

Mikal turned his head to glance first at the hand on his shoulder and then at the grinning face behind it. Was that a knowing male look? What did he mean by 'How was Miss Kramer?' The kid was still getting from place to place on a skateboard, for God's sake. "She was fine when I left her."

"Come on! You know what I mean." David moved around Mikal's chair and sat down across from him. "She's not bad looking, is she?"

Mikal turned his mouth down and paused consideringly. "Not bad at all."

"Did you make any bases with her?" David wondered anxiously.

"Bases? You mean as in baseball or air force?"

Mikal's knee got a punch. "Come on, Dad. You know what I mean."

"What kind of bases are you running these days?" David's knee got a return punch.

"It's soccer season."

"Aerobics season, from what I understand."

"Well, yeah. It's good for the respiratory system." David grinned broadly. There was no such thing as a genuine sheepish grin among the Romanov men.

"How come you didn't ask me to buy you a leotard?"

"Geez, you're a tease." It was a rhyme they offered back and forth, and it was always accompanied by another playful punch. "You're not gonna tell me anything, are you?"

"I'll tell you that I had a nice evening and thank you for selling me that ticket."

David nodded, smiling. "Want a sandwich?"

"Sure." Mikal followed David's retreat to the kitchen and shot him another question as an afterthought. "Does Miss Kramer wear a leotard in aerobics class?"

It was a hazy fantasy that danced across Mikal's mind in the days that followed. Morgan Kramer in a leotard. Morgan Kramer—whom he'd seen outfitted only in crisp, high-necked propriety—jumping around to music, sweating and stretching like the exercise fanatics on TV. When David called home to say he'd forgotten his gym shorts and needed them next hour for phys ed, Mikal grinned as he hung up the phone.

David grinned back when he saw his father in the gym lobby. Mikal produced the shorts from the pocket of his jacket, and David snatched them on the run. "Gotta go, Dad. Thanks!"

Mikal watched his son melt into the flow of chattering adolescent traffic in the hallway. One bell sounded, and the halls cleared quickly. Another bell warned the two girls who burst forth from the bathroom that they were late. Mikal smiled, aware of his own impulse to move at the sound of the bell. He figured he'd give her about ten minutes. By then the class should be under way.

An alcove inside the gym gave him the advantage of being able to watch without being readily noticeable. Rock music filled the room to the rafters, and forty kids, mostly girls, followed their instructor's lead, jumping, toe-touching, hustling and hopscotching in time to the music. Her leotard was black, trimmed in pink, and it topped shiny black tights and pink leg-warmers, bunched near her ankles. She wore a pink headband, and her hair was caught up in a ponytail that swayed and bounced as she led the group through a routine with her back to the alcove where Mikal stood.

"And it's punch...punch...punch. Now, reach, two, three, four. And punch. Reach it out. Stretch the waist. Stretch the back. And tabletop. Flat back. Knees bent, touch the floor. Grab the ankles, drop the head..."

With her head hanging somewhere below her knees, her ponytail sweeping the floor, blood rushing to her brain, and bottom uppermost, she saw him. He smiled and fluttered his fingers at her. Even upside-down, his smile was charming. Morgan missed a beat, but only one. "Nose to knee. Other nose—other *knee*—and roll it up."

Between songs she stopped the tape. "Mr. Romanov, you're welcome to come and join us!"

He gave a quick laugh. "David forgot his gym shorts. I just thought I'd take a peek."

"We love to have parents observe, Mr. Romanov, but we always try to include them in the activity." Extending her hand in invitation, she flashed him a bright smile before turning to her class. "In fact, we insist, don't we?" The chorus of "Yeah, come on!" masked Morgan's mumbled, "You should've picked social studies. You could've gotten away with listing the countries in Africa." She'd already pulled him several feet into the gym.

"But I'm not . . ." Mikal looked down at the sweats and running shoes that he spent many comfortable hours in and realized that he *was* dressed for this. He rolled his eyes toward the ceiling and shucked his jacket. That got him scattered applause.

"We're just getting started," Morgan said, placing Mikal in the group, front and center. "Do a little of this." She demonstrated a couple of stretches, and he followed suit. "Now go at your own pace. When your pulse rate gets too high, just jog in place."

*"When?"* Mikal figured that the gauntlet had been thrown. "Let's have some music, Miss Kramer."

Mikal was a good dancer, and he was in the habit of running every day, but he found himself flagging as the increased pace had them ponying out of one song and goose-stepping into the next. He noted that Morgan Kramer was, indeed, sweating, but she was smiling, shouting instructions and smiling again. Mikal's side began to ache, but he'd be damned if he'd let her show him up. He took a swipe at the perspiration trickling down his face and smiled back.

Just when he thought they must be finished, the kids ran for a pile of rubberized mats, and the floor exercises began. Mikal did sit-ups and crunches and bicycles until he thought his gut would split, but as long as

Morgan kept smiling, he managed to smile back. The fire-hydrant kicks seemed undignified, as did the pelvic lifts. He decided that this woman couldn't count past eight, but she knew one through eight forward and backward, and she counted up and down forever just for practice while he strained his every muscle.

"And it's squeeze, squeeze, squeeze..."

Mikal stifled a groan. If he ever got his arms around her, he would do just that.

"And lift, lift, lift..."

Give me a chance, lady. I can do that, too.

"Make it work. Make it burn. Keep it up."

The woman was indefatigable. Or was she insatiable? He looked up and grinned past the sweat that threatened to stream into his eyes. Again she smiled back, her face bright with mischief, and he decided that she was probably equal parts of both. It might be worth taking the time to find out.

"One more set. And it's *one*-two-three-four-five-six-seven-eight, *two*-two-three..."

After the students had cleared the gym, Morgan offered Mikal a towel, which he accepted gratefully. "That's pretty good exercise," he admitted, mopping his face.

"You approve of David's choice, then?"

"Heartily." He flipped the towel over his shoulder and leaned against a wall of bleachers. "And after a workout like that, you should be able to eat as much as you want. How about dinner tonight?"

Morgan looked up, surprised. "Dinner?"

"At my place. I'm a great cook."

"I'm sure you are." Morgan glanced away and shook her head quickly. "I'm afraid I'm busy tonight."

"Tomorrow night, then."

"Um . . . no. There's a basketball game. I'll have to be here for . . . Thank you, but I can't."

Mikal considered her face for a moment, searching it for the real reasons. When she didn't offer any, he shrugged and returned her towel. "Some other time maybe. Let me know if you're ever free." He picked up his jacket, slung it over his shoulder and offered his charming smile in parting. "Thanks for the workout."

Morgan had dinner alone that night. In solitude she sipped her after-dinner coffee and read the evening paper. At least, she made an attempt to read it. Nothing sank in. The silence in the living room was deafening, and the room she'd designed for coziness and comfort suddenly seemed cold. Why had she turned down his invitation? She'd enjoyed herself with him before, and she'd thought about him a great deal since that evening.

Too much. She'd thought about him daily, almost hourly, and that was more than she could handle. He was charming, she reminded herself, and she was being sucked right in by that charm. He was a dreamer, and the world needed a few dreamers to furnish its ideals. The world also needed a good supply of down-to-earth workers to keep its gears moving from one day to the next. Morgan was a worker. She was productive and practical. This dreamer was a distraction, nothing more.

As she turned the page of the newspaper, an advertisement caught Morgan's eye. "Awareness Rally. Freedom International. Twenty-Four Hour Candlelight Vigil." It sounded like something out of the sixties. Aging hippies trying to raise a consciousness that had all but gone to sleep in this day and age. Mikal would be at the forefront, and almost no one would pay any attention. In fact, she couldn't remember there ever having been much interest in Bismarck, except perhaps among the "transplants" from the east. Dakota prairie-dwellers' feet were, much like her own, firmly rooted in prairie sod.

Strangely she felt embarrassed for Mikal. "My dad's weird," David had said, and she wondered if he were embarrassed, too. She remembered the look on David's face when his father had joined the aerobics class, a look of pure delight. She would have expected embarrassment from a thirteen-year-old whose father had appeared in his exercise class, but there was none. "Awareness Rally," she read again, and made a mental note of the time and place.

## Chapter Three

The fact that the auditorium was more than half-filled surprised Morgan. Apparently Mikal Romanov the writer was a respectable drawing card. Or perhaps some of the town was more "aware" than she had suspected. She took a chair at the back of the room as she wondered whether dreamers were born as often as the proverbial suckers. She hoped there would always be enough cynics like herself around to keep things on an even keel.

Within moments she had picked up the thread of the speech in progress. A man with a professional bearing was delineating the effects of apartheid in South Africa, punching a finger at the air as he delivered point after point. Passion for his subject and total self-absorption marked the man as a teacher, probably a college professor, Morgan thought.

As she craned her neck to survey the crowd, she recognized several professors from the local college, some clergymen, some young people who were probably students, and a few stray passersby, but she didn't see Mikal. Several people were taking notes, while others sipped coffee from Styrofoam cups, one man clipped his nails, and another read. Some listened with interest, others with ire. Morgan chafed in her chair, not because she didn't agree with the speaker's condemnation of the apartheid system, but because she couldn't share his passion. She jumped in surprise when someone touched her shoulder.

Mikal smiled, enjoying the unguarded expression he'd caught on her face. "Glad you could come," he whispered.

"I can't stay, really. I just . . ."

"That's okay. You can always come back later. We've got some great speakers, and there are some people here I want you to meet. We've got about eighteen hours to go." He squeezed her shoulder. "See you later."

She watched him make his way to the front of the room as the speaker finished his remarks. Mikal claimed the audience's attention with a few words. The words themselves were not surprising, since he was only introducing another speaker, but the rich depth of his voice, his smooth delivery and the way he commanded the space he occupied drew all eyes and ears. Morgan sensed that she was not alone in her disappointment when another speaker claimed the microphone.

After a talk about an imprisoned Soviet dissident and another on political prisoners in the Middle East, a break was announced. Morgan made her way toward the door.

"Could I interest you in some lunch?"

She turned toward the sound of Mikal's voice and found him standing beside her with a half-eaten sandwich in one hand. He'd shed the sports jacket he'd been wearing and looked more himself in his brown corduroy pants and yellow sweater. Morgan glanced back at the exit door.

"We've got excellent baloney," Mikal said.

"I have no doubt of that." Her plans for the afternoon became insignificant the moment he smiled and beckoned her his way. She followed him into a small anteroom, where an urn of fresh coffee was being brewed. That much, she admitted to herself, was tempting.

The refrigerator in the corner yielded a sandwich, and there were trays piled high with cookies on one of the tables. Morgan took a paper plate and reached for the sandwich, but Mikal raised a teasing eyebrow and cocked his head toward a coffee can labeled Donations Accepted.

"I warned you," Mikal said. "At a rally you're fair game." He held the sandwich in front of her face. "How much is a choice cut of baloney worth to you, Miss Kramer?"

"I have a feeling this is a double-sided coin. Is this your own personal baloney, Mr. Romanov?"

His eyes danced. "Made from my own home-grown bull."

"So that's what I'm about to be fed." Morgan laughed, shaking her head as she fished inside her purse. "What I'm about to *pay* to be fed." She added her money to the coffee can and took the sandwich. "I don't even like baloney."

"You'll like mine."

"Do me one favor?" she asked as she added a brownie to her plate. She glanced his way and added another dollar to the can. "Don't tell me about the starving children who'd give anything for this nutritious baloney sandwich."

"You've seen them for yourself."

The Styrofoam cup was already in her hand. With a sigh, she dipped into her purse again and let him see that she took the last of her cash from her wallet and deposited it in the can before she filled the cup with coffee.

Mikal laughed. "You're too easy."

"Once a missionary's kid, always a missionary's kid." She eyed him over the rim of her cup and saw that he was studying her in a way that made her uneasy. "You're right, of course. I *have* seen them."

"Freedom International isn't about starving children. It's about prisoners and hostages."

"Some people deserve to be imprisoned." Morgan took a seat on the vinyl couch near the refrigerator, and Mikal helped himself to a cup of coffee before joining her.

"After a fair trial and a conviction, some people do. We're talking about people who are imprisoned because they're black or Jewish or the wrong kind of Muslim, or because they disagree with the people in power."

"People like your uncle who was left behind."

"That's right," Mikal agreed, hooking an arm over the back of the couch as he settled in to relax. "People like him. I want you to meet my uncle Yuri." He smiled, and his affection for his uncle glistened in his eyes. "He's quite a character. He's been all over the world, and he has some terrific stories to tell." He cocked his head at another thought. "I'll bet your father has some, too. I'd like to meet him."

"Maybe it's your uncle and my father who should get together," Morgan suggested. "I doubt that I need to be in on any of this. I have no dreams of saving the world."

"You're doing your part. You were pretty intent on saving my kid."

He gave her a look that said he knew more about her than she did, and she swallowed a quick protest. It occurred to her that kids didn't like that look much, either, and she knew she'd used it on them. "I do my job. I'm not unrealistic about it, though. I'm in the business of educating, not saving."

"Semantics." With a wave of his hand, he dismissed the difference. "No one person can save the world, but each of us can play his part to improve the chances of its survival. Yours is with kids. And you're good at it; I know, because I've watched you."

She knew she was being charmed by a professional. Ordinarily she would take exception to being winked at, but when Mikal did it, she smiled and warmed to the compliment. "Will we see how good you are at what you do?" she asked. "I came to hear you speak."

Mikal glanced at his watch. "Stick around, then. I think I'm about out of history professors." He took a small book from the pocket of his jacket, which he left hanging on a coatrack in the corner of the room, then motioned for Morgan to join him.

Morgan headed for the rear of the room but Mikal steered her to the front with a firm hand. From her previous seat in the back she hadn't noticed the table full of large white candles, twenty-four in all. Eight of them were already aflame, and Mikal struck a match to light the ninth one before he went to the podium. He opened the small book and read.

It was poetry—stunning, offered without fanfare, without credits, without explanatory transition between pieces. Morgan had anticipated hearing Mikal's thoughts, or perhaps some anecdotes about his uncle Yuri, who was obviously one of the movement's mentors. Ideas and anecdotes she could contend with, but she didn't like poetry. It was like music; it came too close to getting under her skin. The writer behind the little book in Mikal's hands exposed too much of himself. Morgan resisted the first three poems, listening only with her intellect, but the fourth took hold of something else inside her, something she guarded jealously.

The poem spoke of being touched by harsh hands, and it evoked images of pain, then numbness. It spoke of separation and want of company. Finally it offered the poet's touch, a caring touch to soothe the mind and heal the spirit. "Don't shut me out," the poet entreated in Mikal's gentle voice. "Let me shed my tears upon your feet and dry them with my hair."

And there were more poems. Mikal Romanov, a writer himself, chose to read poetry rather than to speak his own prose. It was effective, Morgan admitted to herself. He chose poems that spoke of the despair found only in isolation and of the human heart's capacity for compassion. She wondered at the man. He appeared to be the image of masculinity, yet there was such softness in his message. What would he know of tears? Was this the most subtle refinement of his charm?

The audience stood to applaud, but Morgan came to her feet more slowly than the rest. When Mikal left the podium, she followed, curious about the small book in his hand. It was the book she followed, really, and when he finally stopped and turned to her, she reached for it without explanation. None was needed, and he handed it to her.

*Breath of Freedom.* Mikal Romanov. Morgan looked up and found him waiting for her comment. "That was your own poetry?" She studied the book cover again. "I thought you were a novelist."

"I am. At least, that's what I get paid for. I like to think I'm a poet, too, but not for money."

"For what, then?"

"For love." He nodded toward the book in her hand. "Proceeds from the sale of that book go to Freedom International."

Impulsively she drew it to her breast. "Where's the coffee can?"

"The book is yours."

"Oh, no, I want to pay for it."

"You don't have any money left, remember?" He smiled. "You gave all you had, Miss Kramer. That makes you entitled to charity. That book is my charity."

"Thank you." Morgan looked down at the book again, still holding it close. She was glad it wasn't returnable. The word "charity" took on new meaning, making her heart feel light. "So how's it going so far?"

Mikal raised a quizzical brow. "You mean the rally?"

Nodding, Morgan surveyed the auditorium lobby. One man was perusing the literature on a display table, and two women were talking in the far corner of the room. "Does something like this really bring in very much money?"

"The purpose of something like this is to make people aware of the injustices that abound in this world."

Her light heart wanted to giggle at his seriousness. "Really, Mikal, we're sitting in the middle of Bismarck, North Dakota. What have we got to say about what goes on in South Africa or Siberia?''

He loved that question. It was his cue to take her by the elbow, steer her over to the table and shove a fat paperback book into her hands. "We say we don't like it," he insisted. "We say we won't stand for torture or capital punishment, and when somebody gets locked up, somebody else better have a damn good reason—''

"Who's listening to us, Mikal?'' Morgan noted that the man who'd been standing at the table was listening, as were the other two women, and she sobered, lowering her voice, "Opening the window and shouting 'I'm mad as hell' doesn't seem to scare the Kremlin.''

"You'd be surprised. One voice may not mean much, but you add your voice to mine, and we'll be twice as loud. We write letters by the thousands, and somebody reads them." He tapped a finger on the book he'd just handed her. "Read this and see how it works.''

"Sounds like a lotta pinko bull to me.''

Mikal glanced up, and Morgan turned toward the man who'd been sorting through pamphlets at the other end of the table. He was about Mikal's height, perhaps a few years younger, but he carried some extra weight in a belly that hung over his belt like a pouch. He eyed Mikal with dark suspicion.

"I seen you on TV talking about the missile site they want to build. Whose side are you on, anyway?'' The man's nose, already red, seemed to darken as his face flushed with angry color. He edged closer to Mikal. "This here's the U.S. of A., and we carry a big stick. I say shoot first and ask questions later." The gum in the man's mouth snapped when he grinned. "What do you say?"

Morgan stepped back involuntarily, but Mikal seemed completely at ease, even offering the man his hand. "Mikal Romanov. I didn't catch your name."

Mikal's hand was ignored. "I didn't give it. I'm here to tell you you sound like a sissy. You want the rest of the country thinkin' we got a bunch of sissies out here in North Dakota? I went to Nam. I did my duty. Did you?"

"I...did my duty, yes. I'm doing it now. Look, maybe we should talk about this—"

Mikal's hand-on-the-shoulder gesture was shrugged off, and the man bristled. "You got something against keeping America strong, mister? What in hell's wrong with you? You look like a man, but you talk like a woman." He poked at Mikal's shoulder with his forefinger, and Morgan stiffened as she watched, her nails digging into her palms. Talk like a woman—was that the ultimate insult? "You're scared of everything, aren't you? Scared of Nam, scared of nukes." Mikal held his ground as the man experimented with a harder tap. "Scared of me? Huh?"

"I'd be glad to—" The man had no interest in what would make Mikal glad. It was Mikal's hand on his arm that interested him, and that for only a moment before he punched Mikal in the jaw.

Morgan gasped as Mikal stepped back for balance, raising a hand to his cheek. "You good for anything but talk, Mister Peacenik? Huh?"

Mikal dodged a second punch and caught the man's arm on the third try. "You need to cool off, friend," Mikal said quietly as he moved the man toward the door. "Anytime you want to talk, we'll talk, but I won't fight with you."

"Yeah, that's what I thought. Talk's cheap, mister. Take your hands—"

"But fighting's too expensive." Mikal moved the man through the door using, as far as Morgan could tell, nothing more than a hold on his arm. When Mikal returned, he was rubbing his jaw and shaking his head. He caught Morgan's concerned look and gave her half a smile. "Could have been worse. I've got a steel jaw and a glass nose."

"I guess it's a good thing you didn't hit him back, then," she said, craning her neck for a closer look at his jaw.

"Disappointed?" He moved his jaw from side to side a couple of times, and she heard it crack.

"Of course not. Are you okay?"

"I think everything's back in place."

"Aren't you going to call the police?"

"Not unless he comes back." The incredulous look on her face made him laugh. "You're thinking the script should've called for me to take at least one parting shot at him once I got him outside. You like John Wayne movies?"

"Not particularly." Morgan smiled. "I prefer Woody Allen."

"Me, too." But I like your smile even more, he thought. He decided she'd spend this night with him even though they'd have to share it with a cause less sensual than the one that had nagged him ever since he'd first laid eyes on her legs. "I don't suppose you brought your leotard along?"

"My leotard?"

"I've got a job for you."

He touched her, and Morgan lifted her chin, listening. His hand on her shoulder made it impossible for her to do less, and she wasn't inclined to shrug it off. She had a feeling that before the night was over she would learn that once Mikal Romanov had a listener, chances were he had a new sympathizer for the cause.

Morgan wasn't ready to distribute pamphlets, but the job Mikal gave her didn't require any soul-searching. Keeping the participants alert by leading them in a little exercise seemed a small request. A leotard was hardly necessary. Her red blouse was soft and comfortable, and she'd worn loose-fitting slacks. All she asked for was some music and some floor space. It seemed a little silly to start her session by lighting the fifteenth candle, but Mikal insisted that it was part of the tradition. As she led the exercises, she looked to the back of the room and caught him stretching to the right when she'd said left. She smiled when he switched.

He looked up, grinning, and gave her a helpless shrug. So what if he was too tired to remember which side was the left? He'd gotten Morgan Kramer to light a candle.

The numbers had thinned to a few of the hardiest and most dedicated by the wee hours of morning. Morgan told herself she qualified for hardy and dedicated, though not necessarily to this cause. As the crowd diminished in size, the speeches became discussions. Morgan found herself enjoying the people she met and becoming interested in their views. There was even a sing-along. By request, Mikal read more poetry, and Morgan took out her copy of the book and followed his words. She was drawn to his compassion because he spoke of more than the isolation of the physical prisoner. He decried the mental prisons that plagued all human lives.

The end of the vigil came too quickly for Morgan, and when most of the others had left, she sat near the front of the auditorium and watched twenty-four bobbing flames. The first few candles had to be replaced after they'd burned down. Her father had loved to use candles in his churches, and she remembered making them with her mother for Christmas once. It had been a sultry Advent season that year, and all the candles, improperly stored, had melted. She remembered thinking it was too hot to make candles, but Mother had said it wouldn't be Christmas without them.

"What would you usually be doing this early on a Sunday morning?"

Morgan looked up quickly. Mikal lowered himself to the floor and settled, cross-legged, next to her. The mention of regular Sunday activity aroused a deep-seated vestige of guilt in her brain. Years ago she'd risen earlier on Sunday than any other day. "Sleeping," she confessed.

"How about breakfast?"

"I couldn't even scramble a decent egg at this point."

"Neither could I. Let's go catch the sunrise and then find a pancake house," he suggested.

"I'm broke," she reminded him.

Mikal checked his pocket. "I'm not, which just goes to prove that when you give all you have—"

"It turns up in somebody else's pocket."

He shook his head. "You'll be provided for somehow."

"Where's David?" Morgan asked.

"At his Aunt Peg's." He turned his eyes toward the row of candles. "Sleeping. We'll roust him out and take him along."

Morgan nodded, but she said, "It's too soon to roust him yet, though."

"Yes, you're right. Not before sunrise. There's no need to rush."

Mikal waited, wondering what was on her mind. She was a private woman. Hauntingly beautiful, to be sure, but that wasn't what drew him to her. She tried to keep her beauty private. All of it. She bound her feelings as she bound her hair, and Mikal's hands itched to set both of them free.

"How often do you see your uncle Yuri?"

"As often as he can manage," Mikal told her. "Maybe three or four times a year, maybe not even that. I wish it could be more." He let her consider that piece of personal information for a moment and then he asked, "How often do you see your father?"

"Not often at all. The older he gets, the more desperate he seems about his work. He takes so little time for himself."

"And for you?"

She was quiet for a moment. "I'm a grown woman. A father isn't a crucial factor in my life."

"Anymore," he added for her. "You could visit him. You have free time in the summer."

"He asks me to do that every year." She sighed as she poked her finger into a warm bit of melted wax at the base of a candle. "But he has his children, and I have mine."

"Maybe you're both more desperate about your work as the time passes."

Morgan frowned, considering, and then she shook her head quickly, wondering how she could give such a thought any credence at all. Fatigue, she decided. "I have sensible, attainable goals. There's no reason for me to be desperate."

"I see. Do I seem desperate to you?"

"No," she admitted. The commitment was there, but his demeanor was never anything but casual.

"How about my goals? Do they strike you as sensible and attainable?"

"I guess I don't see how they can be."

"And I guess I think they'd better be or we're all in a lot of trouble." He smiled and shrugged. "But I may not see them realized, not in my lifetime. The man who designed Notre Dame Cathedral didn't see his project finished, either. He knew it would take a hundred years to build, but that didn't stop him from giving it all he had."

"But he was working on something tangible. He could control the mortar and stone, put it where he wanted it, make it amount to something. My father and your uncle—" she looked at him steadily "—and you, Mikal Romanov, you're all off on a canoe trip, and you haven't got a paddle. Even if you make a little headway, the current's bound to shift, and you'll be back where you started. You can't really change anything. You don't have access to the right buttons."

"Do you?"

"I don't claim to be able to push any buttons."

"When David was in trouble, you called me. Didn't you think I was the right button? I can't make David learn, any more than you can. All we can do is try to shed some light on the choices, offer some awareness." Mikal moved closer. He closed his hands over Morgan's arms, his eyes never leaving hers. His voice was a soft, warm sound within the darkened room. "How much control do we have, Morgan? Kids have ideas of their own. Laws change. Governments topple overnight. Mortar cracks."

The candlelight flickered in Mikal's eyes, and Morgan was mesmerized. She struggled for words, any words. "We can control ourselves. We can make our decisions rationally, based on—"

"I've decided to kiss you," he said, lowering his head. "I'll try to do it rationally."

She watched his mouth's slow descent until she felt his breath on her face, and then she let her eyes drift shut. There was no question of turning away, even though some stubborn thing inside her protested as she lifted her chin for the tentative touch of his lips to hers. It was his kiss, his message, his gift to her. He pulled her closer and gave more deeply, and she accepted. By nature he was generous, and she was reserved. It was all she could do at the moment just to accept. His kiss tasted of the promise that he had so much to give to someone who could give in return, and her heart drummed out the words "I can do it," while her brain flashed "Control" in red warning lights.

Mikal could almost hear the argument he knew was going on inside Morgan's head, but her lips felt warm against his and her mouth tasted sweet. It had been years since he'd tasted anything so sweet this early in the morning. She revived him with a quick rush of energy, and he wished he had the power to transport them somewhere else. The hell with being rational. He slid one hand up to her shoulder, then to her neck, folding his fingers around the back of her head to hold her still.

"How's that for rational?" he whispered against her lips.

"Not so good," she managed. "But as kisses go, it was superb."

"It was controlled, believe me." He sat back and smiled. "Raised a little awareness in you, though, didn't it?" She glanced away, and he chuckled. "Raised mine, too. Shall we make a wish and blow out the candles?"

Morgan looked to the twenty-four bright flames, the sole source of light in the dark, empty auditorium. The room was forbidding, except for the warm space she shared with Mikal in the candlelight. Her one wish at that moment was to keep the candles burning.

The sky was beginning to lighten when Mikal pulled the car off the road onto a bluff above a lazy bend in the Missouri River. The sign said that Fort Lincoln State Park was closed for the season, but Mikal wasn't interested in reconstructed blockhouses or earth lodges. He was interested in the painted prairie sky and the reflection of dawn drifting in the water below. Zipping up the jacket he'd taken from the backseat, he opened the door on the passenger's side and reached for Morgan's hand.

"Should we be here?" she asked in a hushed tone. Gravel ground too loudly underfoot, and the slamming of the car door announced their intention to trespass. "The police hang out here—" she lowered her voice quickly as if conspiring to commit some mischief "—waiting for speeders."

"And parkers," he whispered. "But we're neither."

"The car *is* parked...." She glanced back over her shoulder as she allowed him to lead her up a grassy hill. Dry leaves crackled under her shoes.

"We're not in it." He picked up his pace once they reached higher ground. "So we're not parkers. Am I going too fast for you?"

"Not at all," she said as she doubled her steps to keep up with his long-legged stride. Heavens, yes, he was going too fast for her, but she seemed to be moving at the same pace.

"Then we're not speeders."

"But the park is closed," she whispered. "I don't think we're supposed to..." Her step never faltered as she followed his lead.

"There's a spot over here, just beyond the buffalo berry bushes."

A fine, white mist hugged the riverbanks as night receded and soft light claimed the jagged horizon. Morgan stood beside Mikal, their breath shooting out in small, white puffs into the vastness of a high-plains morning while they drank deeply of pine-scented air. The river reflected the pink-and-orange sky and made it ripple and shimmer in late fall's last hurrah. In the distance stood barren buttes, deep purple shadows against the expectant sky. Off to the right the river stretched southward, its tree-lined banks cutting a ribbon of contrasts through the grassland. The city lay to the left, lights blinking. In those fragile moments, soft blue haze sifted through the valley like powder. Then crimson cracks widened in the sky and its seams were split by the rays of the rising sun.

Morgan shivered, and Mikal put his arm around her shoulders. She felt tucked-in and cozy, and she slipped her hand beneath his jacket and held him at the waist. "I don't feel like I'm trespassing," she said quietly.

He smiled as he unzipped his jacket. "You aren't. In fact—" he took her hands and slid them under his jacket, directing them around his back "—if your hands are cold, come inside and let me warm them for you."

She spread her fingers and felt the cabled pattern of his sweater. She wanted time to count the cotton stitches under her palms. "It's beautiful here, Mikal."

Gone was the coolness he'd once seen in those hazel eyes. Gold and green glinted in them now, the two shades rivaling one another for dominance like precious gems in neighboring settings. Dazzled, he closed his eyes and pulled her close, tucking her shoulders under his arms and laying his cheek against her hair. "Stay as long as you like," he murmured.

"I mean..." She couldn't let herself say what she meant. The warmth of his body was beautiful, and the intimacy of sharing the space inside his jacket was beautiful, and it would take her hours to count the stitches and memorize the heady scent of his skin. "I mean this spot. But it might be embarrassing if someone catches us here."

"I'll keep a lookout," he promised.

"Perfect place for a lookout," she observed, burying her nose in his jacket's pile lining.

"That's what the Mandan Indians said when they were packing the dirt over log frames to make their lodges here."

"And probably what the soldiers said when they put up their blockhouses."

He could see for miles, and he knew that if he climbed to the top of the hill that stood at his back, he could see forever. High places gave him a sense of power, and holding this woman in his arms put the depths of his feelings in touch with the height of his strength. He sensed that others had been here before him, holding their women, watching the hills change color and relishing the vitality of it all.

"The soldiers had it tough here," he mused. "Of course, Custer and the other officers had their wives with them, but the ordinary soldiers..." He looked across the river at a place where the traders might have peddled their rotgut whiskey. "They'd cross the river and get drunk to try to ward off the loneliness. Sometimes they drowned trying to get back, or they died of alcohol poisoning."

Morgan glanced up, then followed his gaze to the mist-shrouded trees across the river. "I don't suppose there was much for them to do besides watch and wait."

"And listen to the wind," he said. "It's good to keep busy when you're..." He caught himself as he'd learned to do whenever he felt melancholy, and he put those thoughts aside. He was in touch with life and the strength of the hills and Morgan. Her dark brown hair was smooth and soft, pinned to the back of her head and glistening with hints of naughty red in the early-morning sun. "It's good to be here with you," he told her, and he lifted his hands to the back of her head.

"Mikal..." she whispered quickly. But she didn't move away. She felt secure with her hair in its coil, but there was a coil in her stomach, too. It relaxed a notch each time he spoke, each time he touched her.

"Let me," he insisted. "It's morning; time to comb it out. Let me do that." He used his fingers, and the long, brown hair slipped through them like water—soft and cool. His breath caught in his chest, and he kissed her hard, her hair clutched in his hands.

Her lips trembled when he released them. Her breath came quickly; her eyes were closed. "We should go before..."

"Yes," he assured her, touching her cheek. "We have to get back."


David wished his dad would go away and let him sleep. He and his uncle Bill had been up half the night working on the computer. Dad was always hyped up after an all-night rally, and he always wanted to talk. David wanted to rest. He wanted to scrunch down deep and wallow in the luxury of sleeping in. He wasn't interested in food, either. He wasn't interested in...

"Miss Kramer?" David lowered the covers from his face. "What was she doing there?"

"Just curious, I guess. But she got hooked. You and I are taking her out to breakfast."

"Hooked? Miss Kramer?" David braced himself on his elbows as his jeans landed across his legs.

"Well, she stayed to the end. I'd say that was hooked. Wouldn't you?"

"I'd say she might be interested, but I wouldn't count on her being hooked already. She's pretty cagey." David swung his feet over the side of the bed and reached for his jeans. He knew darn well they were talking about two different interests and two different kinds of "hooked," but that wasn't important. What *was* important was that . . . "Is she here now?"

"She's downstairs talking to Aunt Peg." Mikal sat on the bed and braced his palms on his knees. "What do you mean by cagey?"

"Well, you know—pretty sharp. Like you can't put anything over on her." As he zipped his jeans, David took a quick survey of his father's yellow pullover and cords. "Don't you have anything better than that to wear?"

Mikal had to look down to remember what he'd put on almost a day and a half earlier. "What's wrong with this? It's comfortable."

David picked up a comb and answered Mikal's reflection in the mirror. "That's the problem, Dad. You look too comfortable. Adults are supposed to look starched. You know what I mean?"

David's shirt, hanging neatly over the back of a chair, caught Mikal's eye and he nodded thoughtfully. Peg had undoubtedly ironed the shirt and put it there for him the night before. At home David was responsible for his own laundry, and he often did

Mikal's, as well. "I know what you mean. But I'm not starched, and I doubt if I can convince Miss Kramer that I am." He smiled. "What with her being so cagey and all."

"I guess not." He tossed the comb, then grinned when Mikal caught it. "Maybe she'd settle for neat and clean."

"Maybe she would."

## Chapter Four

He marked the days on the wall
small scratches in gray cement
The man who had warned the world
the voice of the voiceless
Alone, undernourished, he could have survived
The cold, the damp, the lash could not kill him
But for want of paper and pencil
He starved

Morgan closed the book and set it aside. Not satisfied, she tossed a magazine over it and picked up the
newspaper. It had been days since she'd read the paper thoroughly. She was shirking her duty to keep
herself informed, and all because of that little book.

She'd read it and reread it, but it kept drawing her again. She had to get back on track.

"Diplomat Disappears in Middle East." "Senate Debates Arms Sale." "Assassination in Latin America." "Unrest on the Island of De Colores." De Colores? Her father was there. How could there be unrest on an island paradise? Why not? Morgan asked herself, flipping to another page. There was trouble everywhere else. Trouble in Bismarck. "School Board Divided Over Building Proposal." Morgan sighed, turning the page again. She'd be in an overcrowded building forever. "Dow Jones Up." Sure. Somebody was making money on all this misery.

Somebody was... Morgan closed the newspaper. She had to be careful. She was even beginning to think like Mikal. Not that she *disagreed* with him, but passive agreement on distant issues was enough. It was the school board's decision that affected her. Those other things were just food for thought. Active agreement with Mikal could mean...action. And to what end? Mikal hadn't published anything in five years. He was totally impractical.

He was disturbing. His poetry had become a fixation for her. He knew people's minds. He knew the imprisoned dissident who died because he couldn't write. He knew the exile, the refugee, the immigrant. And he knew loneliness. He'd called her once since the rally and invited her to dinner, but she'd been busy so the invitation had been left open. She wondered if he was aware of her loneliness. She regarded it as a private matter, but he knew people's minds, and it disturbed Morgan that he might know hers.

There was absolutely nothing in the refrigerator worth eating, and there was absolutely no restaurant in town worth going to tonight. Morgan's stomach was empty. She was actually hungry, and she had an open invitation for dinner. She called Mikal.

"Come on in. We'll put you to work." Mikal's once-white butcher's apron hung from his neck like a knee-length bib, covering jeans and a fisherman's-knit sweater. Morgan handed him her coat and checked her watch. "We started without you, but we're not very far along. Find a place for this, David."

She watched her coat go from hand to hand, returned David's greeting, then checked her watch again. She was on time. "Started without me?"

"We're working on the crepes." Mikal took another apron from a drawer, shook it out and draped it over Morgan's head. "You haven't missed much." Turning her around by the shoulders, he leaned close to her ear, chuckling while he tied the apron around her waist. "You weren't expecting to be waited on, were you?"

"I expected to get here in time for the first course."

"You did. Would I deny you the best part of a meal?"

"Dessert?"

"Preparation! You want to know what you're eating, don't you?"

Morgan sniffed the air, which was tangy with the smell of tomato sauce and Italian sausage. It was a smell that went with the kitchen, which was traditional in design and functional in decor. Gleaming copper-bottomed pots and pans were suspended from a rack in the middle of the room, and there was a wooden chopping block, along with crockery and a wide variety of utensils. Individually potted herbs grew in the windowsill. "Spaghetti?"

"Cannelloni. I was sure you wouldn't want to miss flipping the crepes."

Frowning, she thought for a moment. "I don't think I've ever flipped a crepe. But I warn you, I can't turn an egg without breaking the yolk."

"Aha! Raw material," Mikal exclaimed, rolling the words with an unidentifiable foreign accent. With one arm he guided Morgan toward the stove while he gestured flamboyantly with the other. "A pupil to be molded like a soft piece of dough, shaped to my specifications. 'Tis a consummation devoutly to be wished."

"Your wish may be very different after you see what I can do to a pancake." The batter caught her eye, and she took the spoon out of it and watched the thin stuff drip back into the bowl.

Mikal caught her hand. "*Crepes*, not pancakes. Don't tease the batter. See how you make it cry?"

"I think we have a serious case of infantile personification here." Smiling, she laid the back of her hand on his forehead. "Any other symptoms?"

"Fever?"

"I can feel a twinge, yes," she decided.

"This could ruin my career. Any suggestions?"

"Bite your tongue when you feel another bout coming on."

"The cure could ruin me, as well. On with the crepes?"

"On with the crepes. What's my assignment?"

"Observe, my dear pupil. Let there be fire." Gas flames leaped to life under the crepe pan's round bottom.

"And there was fire," Morgan observed.

David rounded the corner of the island counter and peered past Mikal's shoulder into the pan. "You're in for a treat, Miss Kramer. Dad could turn the soles of your shoes into something delicious."

Without looking up from stirring the batter, Mikal muttered. "Don't give away the chef's secrets."

"I think I *do* want to know what I'm eating."

"Pay no attention to the kid. I haven't done fillet of sole since I got my first book advance."

"No, but you've done leg of frog and arm of octopus," David put in. "Mrs. Kopeke called a while ago and wondered if something was burning up here and why it didn't smell like steak, since it sounds like we have company."

Mikal rolled his eyes toward the ceiling and gave a good-natured chuckle. "Mrs. Kopeke lives in our basement apartment," he told Morgan. "And we're not having steak because it's no challenge. Miss Kramer needs to learn to flip crepes."

"You don't flip crepes?" David asked seriously.

"Uh, no, I haven't . . ."

"You see, David? This kind of deprivation is rampant, even in our own city. Pancakes. That's all they know." Morgan searched for a comeback, but Mikal dismissed the attempt with "We're here to help you, Miss Kramer. Watch carefully."

He used a crepe pan as deftly as most men used a razor. One flick of the wrist and the pan was coated with batter. Another flick of the spatula and the crepe was turned perfectly. A final flick and it was out of the pan. Morgan tried to repeat the process, but with less success. Mikal coaxed her to try again, and she improved with practice. She knew she could never match his dexterity with a chopping knife, and she marveled that nothing was measured before it went into his bowls.

"And now for the sauce béchamel."

Morgan watched Mikal whisk flour and butter together and thought of the many times she'd burned food at this stage. She leaned toward David and put a hand on his shoulder. "I have no idea what he's talking about. Are we on camera? Is this really the 'Galloping Gourmet'?"

David laughed. "Galloping is good. That fits. I thought you adults all spoke the same language."

"I speak pretty good *Franco American*. What's sauce béchamel?"

"A little salt . . . and a pinch of fresh nutmeg." It was not an answer to her question; Mikal was talking to himself—or possibly to his sauce. He tasted. "Perfect."

"How do you keep from getting fat?" Morgan wondered aloud.

"When I'm cooking for four, I make just four servings."

"Four?"

"Mrs. Kopeke," David explained. "Dad's afraid she'll waste away if he doesn't feed her."

"People who live alone don't usually cook for themselves. They start getting—" Mikal glanced at Morgan's small waist "—perilously thin."

"Really?" Morgan's hand went to her flat stomach, and it answered with a growl.

"I think she's perilously hungry, Dad."

Mikal stuck a homemade breadstick in her mouth and invited her to help him stuff crepes. David took care of the table, and when all was ready, he skipped down the stairs with a plate for Mrs. Kopeke.

"What's this stuff?" she was heard to say.

"Cannelloni, Mrs. Kopeke. It's Italian."

"Doesn't he ever make anything Polish?"

"Not if I'm trying to impress somebody," Mikal muttered as he uncorked a bottle of Chianti.

The dry, thin voice at the foot of the stairs ended with, "Well, all right, I guess I can *try* it."

A door closed, and David scampered up the steps. "She's gonna *try* it, Dad." The look that passed between them said this was a ritual they both enjoyed.

Morgan was impressed. Mikal was an artist with food, and the meal was an aesthetic experience. It was something to be savored slowly. "I think *I* would get fat if I ate this way all the time."

"We don't eat this way *all* the time," David said. "Dad makes good sandwiches, too."

"So do you." With obvious satisfaction, Mikal reported, "He's coming along. He makes an excellent hamburger and downright decent pizza."

"You'll be hard-pressed to find a wife who can compete with your father in the kitchen, David," Morgan said as she lifted her wineglass.

"He won't have to. He'll learn to cook the way he wants to eat." Morgan didn't miss the eyebrow Mikal raised in challenge. "Who says the woman has to excel in the kitchen?"

"Certainly not I," Morgan said with a smile.

They heard the door at the foot of the basement steps rattle, then open. "Here's your plate," Mrs. Kopeke shouted from the bottom of the stairs.

David rolled his eyes. "I'll get it," Mikal said as he pushed his chair back from the table. "You start stacking the dishes. I've got plans for Miss Kramer."

"I figured as much," Morgan groaned over her last sip of wine. "If David stacks, I'll wash, and we'll give the cook a break."

"Not dishes. Dancing," Mikal corrected over his shoulder on his way down the stairs. "Did you enjoy that, Mrs. Kopeke?"

"I don't know," the crackling voice replied slowly. "Can't really taste much anymore. Seemed like a funny way to fix pancakes."

"Those were crepes, Mrs. Kopeke, and I'm glad you liked them. How's Oscar?"

Morgan missed the reply because David was filling her in on the facts. "Oscar's a goldfish. Dad just finished wallpapering the kitchen downstairs to cheer Oscar up after Pearl died. Pearl was another goldfish."

"When does your father write?"

"When most people are sleeping. Didn't I tell you he's a saint?" Playing up his father's sainthood seemed to David to be a good idea. Someone like Miss Kramer would be impressed, maybe enough to overlook the obvious...eccentricities. Yes, eccentric sounded better than weird.

Morgan had the dishes organized into neat groups by the time Mikal came back upstairs. "Everything's under control, Mikal, although I should point out that you've used all the bowls and spoons in the place."

"Not possible," David replied. He was letting his nightly chore slip out of his hands, figuring that if Miss Kramer *wanted* to do the dishes, he was in no position to stop her. "We've got every kind of bowl, spoon and pan imaginable."

Mikal stopped in his tracks. "You're letting a guest clean up, David? Your great-grandmother would twist your ears into pretzels." He turned to Morgan. "I said dancing, not dishes."

"Dancing?"

"I want to bop with you, baby." He demonstrated a couple of steps and finally had Morgan laughing.

"If you're talking about the Ray Durkee dance, I heard it's sold out." The disc jockey's annual dance was always well-attended, but Morgan had never found the time to go.

"Ah, but I have tickets. Two." He flashed the number with his fingers.

"You had plans..."

"I had a premonition," he corrected, taking the dish towel from her hand and laying it over David's shoulder. "Is that your best sock-hop outfit? You have to dress the part for Durkee's oldies show."

Morgan reached back to untie the apron she was wearing over a slim charcoal-gray skirt and red blouse. "It's as close as I can get. I wasn't planning—"

"Good! Not planning makes it even better. I'll be ready in two minutes." Backing away, he considered her outfit once more. "I can get closer."

"Closer to what?" Morgan tried, but he had already disappeared down the hallway. At her back she heard a tentative throat-clearing.

"Uh, Miss Kramer...there must be a hundred ways to be weird—I mean *eccentric*—and I think my dad knows them all. He only practices the harmless ones, of course." He shrugged apologetically. "Embarrassing sometimes, but always harmless."

"Maybe it's because he's an artist," Morgan offered, thinking that that excuse didn't give her much comfort. She'd known an artist once before.

"Maybe."

When Mikal came out again he was outfitted as a tall, broad-shouldered version of James Dean. Morgan stifled what threatened to be an adolescent giggle, and he gave her a slow grin. His hair was several shades darker and slicked back in a pompadour. His jeans fit tighter, and his gum popped as he chewed. "Course you realize, this ain't my era, but it's the one I do best. I'm a rebel at heart."

"But *with* a cause." She was close enough to smell the oil in his hair, and she shook her head and laughed.

"Several. One of them is showing you a good time tonight. Ever been to a Durkee dance?" She shook her head again. "Sure you don't want to change clothes?"

"I have absolutely nothing..."

He patted the back of one of the kitchen chairs. "Sit right down here, ma'am. Ain't *nobody* ain't got absolutely *nothin'*."

"That's a double negative." Morgan sat down, realizing that he was doing it again—charming her into doing something crazy.

"Quadruple negative. I think I have a positive there. Got a brush in your purse?" She nodded. "David, where did you put Miss Kramer's purse?"

"I'll get it," David offered, tossing the dish towel aside.

"Have you got a pair of clean white socks, too? And some of that red lipstick you used for that skit you did?" He slid a hairpin from Morgan's upswept hairdo. "Do you mind?"

"Since the answer seems to be no, I now ought to have my head examined."

Mikal smiled at the pleasure he felt in running his fingers through her hair. "I can do that for you while I'm at it. Looks good so far."

As David handed over her purse, she assured him, "You were right the first time. He's weird." But she handed Mikal the brush as though she were in the habit of having her hair styled in his kitchen.

Minutes later he directed her to a full-length mirror, and she stood there in amazement. He'd given her a ponytail, rolled her sleeves just above her elbows, opened the neck of her blouse and added a scarf, and put white socks with her red flats. Then he handed her a tube of lipstick called "Cherries in the Snow." She couldn't resist swishing her ponytail just once before she painted her lips bright red. When Mikal stepped up to the mirror beside her, they both laughed. Then they straightened their faces, looked at one another and laughed even harder. The principal and the poet were going out for the evening.

Nationally syndicated disc jockey Ray Durkee held an annual oldies dance in Bismarck as a benefit for the Association for Retarded Citizens, and Mikal had tickets in support of the cause. The idea of taking Morgan had occurred to him when she'd called to invite herself to his house for dinner, but he'd decided to spring it on her only after he'd plied her with good food and fairly good wine. He knew she was tempted to have fun once in a while, and he'd planned to make the fun start happening before she had time to think about it.

In her "silly outfit" Morgan was free of her staid image. Out on the dance floor she saw people she knew—parents, teachers, her hairdresser, and the couple who lived next door—and she waved gaily. Tonight she was just Morgan. Ray Durkee asked "Remember this one?" and played a vaguely familiar tune. Her feet began to move and soon she was doing steps she thought she'd forgotten long ago. She danced until her blouse stuck to her back and her feet ached from pounding against the cement floor. It was finally Mikal who begged for mercy, and because the disc jockey was taking a break, too, Morgan agreed to sit down.

"I think I've created a monster," Mikal grumbled as they made their way to the end of a long table and reclaimed their folding chairs. "Once you get going, you're unstoppable."

"Making me up to look like the queen of the hop does not make you my creator, Mr. Romanov. This is just another aerobics workout for me." Under the table Morgan slipped her shoes off and flexed her aching toes.

"Not having any fun?" He raised a mocking eyebrow. "I can get you another drink."

She shook her head. "I don't need another drink, and of course I'm having fun. I love a good workout."

"You love to dance. Admit it."

"I love to dance." Her eyes brightened as she smiled with the admission. "And I love dancing with a man who dances well, and you do, so I love dancing with you. But I haven't danced like *this* in years. I feel like a kid!''

The smile he returned held none of the innocence of hers. He leaned closer. ''Great. What do you say we go out in the parking lot and neck?''

It was a joke, of course, but the familiar way he laid his arm along the back of her chair and teased her shoulder with his thumb made her shimmy on the inside just as she had on the outside while she was dancing. ''If you didn't look like such a hood, I might consider it.''

''A hood? Is that better or worse than a hippie?''

''They're probably about even.'' She lifted her hand toward a lock of hair that had fallen over his forehead Presley-style. The look he gave her drew her to touch it, but the hair refused to stay where she placed it. ''Which do you prefer?''

He lifted one shoulder. ''One label's about as bad as the next. How do you like yuppie?''

''Would you call me that?'' she asked, uneasy with the term.

''I'd call you Morgan.'' His hand curved comfortably around her arm. ''And whether you're wearing your hair this way, or all bound up at the back of your head—'' he tilted his head a little to one side, imagining ''—or maybe soft and free, the way it was the other morning, I'd call you a friend of mine. Morgan.'' The name was spoken as a special word. ''Let's go for a walk.''

It was a brisk November night, and the city lights dimmed the stars' brightness. They had only to drive a short distance from town to enjoy the clear, starry sky, but neither suggested it. The crisp air felt good, Morgan thought. It cleared the head and made it seem unwise to pay undue attention to things like stars. Stars, like hair, could get to be sticky subjects.

"Do you smell smoke?"

"Smoke?" Morgan stopped, glancing around quickly.

"I could have sworn you were headed for a fire somewhere. I thought we were going for a walk." Mikal shoved his hands in his pockets and rocked back on the heels of his loafers. "What's it going to be?"

"Just a walk. I'll try to slow down."

He chuckled. "You might as well. Nobody's chasing you." Morgan looked up at him, and he laughed as he put his arm around her shoulders and slowed the pace. "Not that you aren't worth chasing. It's just that I don't think there's any chance of catching you on the run."

"What's that supposed to mean?"

"Every time I ask you out, you shy away. I have better luck if I just plant an idea in your head and wait around until it germinates."

"I don't shy away," Morgan objected, disliking the vision the words suggested of some shrinking violet. "I'm not shy."

"In some ways you are. We make each other nervous." He looked down at her and smiled. "It's kind of a good feeling, isn't it? Kind of anxious and tingly. I haven't felt that kind of nervous in a long time."

They walked in step together, hips nearly touching, as she told herself to relax under his arm so he'd have no reason to be so direct. Their footsteps echoed in the quiet of the night. "Your wife died, didn't she? How long ago?"

"Ten years."

"What happened?" She asked the question gently because she knew the passage of time didn't necessarily mean anything.

"She had leukemia." The words came in a spiritless monotone, filled with a terrible resignation Morgan had never heard before in anything Mikal said. "She was twenty-five."

"And David was only three. What a tragic loss for both of you."

"Yes." He spoke quietly, as though there were something in the night surrounding them that might be disturbed. "I loved her. I might have gone with her if it hadn't been for David." There was a pause. "And for my uncle Yuri."

"Gone with her?"

"In a sense. Not literally, of course, but I didn't want to feel anything anymore. I wanted to stay numb."

"I remember feeling that way when I lost my mother." It hadn't been that long ago, and it was still difficult to use the word "died."

"I didn't lose *her*, really, I just lost out on some time I'd counted on spending with her. At first I wouldn't let it hurt. I told myself to forget and go on with my life. But that didn't work." They had come to an empty parking lot and made a tacit agreement to turn around. Mikal hesitated, and Morgan looked up. "I had to feel the pain and then let it ease up gradually. I had to let her have a piece of my heart, a place where I could carry her comfortably.

"I think you lose somebody when you push them out of your heart, Morgan." He saw that she hadn't made the leap with him yet, from his memories to hers. "Your pride tells you not to give them another chance even though your heart's saving that place for them. Whether they're alive or dead, you'll never be comfortable with that."

Morgan was surprised. He was talking about... "My father?" He nodded. "I haven't pushed him away," she insisted.

"You refuse to see him."

"I don't *refuse* to see him; I just won't go traipsing off to Timbuktu to do it. I saw him... well, I suppose it's been... no more than four or five years."

"Timbuktu's in Africa," he pointed out. "I'd say you were due for a trip to the Caribbean."

She stared at him for a moment. It was true that he made her nervous. Shadows from the streetlights flickered over his face. He looked the part of the brooding rebel, but if this man had been a travel agent, he probably could have sold her a ticket. But she told herself that she didn't want a ticket. "I'd say I'm due for another dance."

They danced until the last record was played. Morgan had left her car at Mikal's house, and he insisted on making coffee for her before she went home.

Though hers was always adequate, she had a feeling his would be excellent, and she wasn't disappointed.

"Where's David?" she asked, following Mikal into the living room. He reached under the shade of a table lamp and clicked on the switch. It was a comfortable room, one that looked as though someone had put it together years ago and it had been lived in ever since. Overstuffed furniture and overstocked bookcases dominated the area.

"He stays at Peg's when I go out for an evening. She's helped us out a lot since Sharon died. She was Sharon's big sister, and then she became mine." He joined her on the sofa. "How's the coffee?"

After another sip she said, "I think it's the best I've ever tasted. You have a secret?"

"Umm-hmm." He smiled, his eyes twinkling. "Lots of them. I don't give them out, because they only work for me."

"What is it? Eggshells? Some kind of spice?" She sipped again and concentrated on the flavor. "I think I taste some spice."

"Magic."

"Come on," she urged. "It isn't cinnamon. It must be..."

He gave an exaggerated sigh. "Believe and enjoy, Morgan Kramer. Magic is a spice that can't be bought or measured."

"Neither can your recipe for cannelloni. Nothing was measured. I don't suppose you could give out a recipe even if you wanted to."

"It's my own magic. What can I tell you?" There was little pretense of modesty in his clear blue eyes. "I can't do much with a hammer and saw, or anything worth a damn under the hood of a car, but in the kitchen I can do no wrong."

Morgan set her cup aside and reached back to take her hair down. "I like your poetry, too," she said, hoping it sounded like no more than a casual compliment. *Like* was hardly an adequate description of the way she felt about his little book.

"You've read it, then?"

She nodded. "Do you have any more?"

"One other volume in print, and sheaves of it that haven't been published. I write poetry when I need to laugh or cry or make a fool of myself over something that seems like a big deal at the time. I sweat over prose, but poetry seems to tumble out of me. I always feel good after I've gotten it out, like I've just done a triple somersault on the trapeze."

"Reading it makes me . . . feel things, too."

He watched her comb her fingers through the dark thickness of her hair. "What kind of things?"

"The things you express," she said as she unrolled one of her sleeves. "Joy, sorrow. Of course, they're really *your* feelings, but they're expressed in such . . . well, I can't help but . . . sympathize."

"I liked the way you said it first." He caught the hand that was fumbling with the buttons on her cuff and fastened them himself as he watched her face. "That it made you feel things. I like that better than 'sympathize.'" He slid his hands down her other arm, unfolding her sleeve as he went. "I like your hair like this, too."

She gave a small, nervous laugh. "Men always seem to like that windblown look."

"Do they?" She didn't object when he lifted one of her feet, slipped her shoe off and slowly peeled away the white sock. "Have you taken a survey?"

"No. The women's magazines do that for us." His fingers skimmed her stockinged foot as he put her shoe back on, and her stomach tightened. "As if we cared."

He switched his attentions to her other foot, but his eyes never left her face. "You have beautiful hair. I had a poet's fantasy about taking the pins out and letting it fall into my hands."

"And what's the difference between a poet's fantasy and any other man's?"

"A poet fantasizes metaphorically. 'Shall I compare thee to a summer's day?'" He dropped the second sock on the floor beside its mate and lowered her foot.

"My hair?" A good, quick comeback escaped her. He was sitting so close to her, and her feet still tingled where he'd touched them.

"I could start there." He touched the smooth hair at her temple and saw that her eyelids lowered just slightly.

"I think you did," she said, struggling to keep the words coming as his hands went to the knot in the scarf around her neck. "Then you went to my feet. What would you compare them to?"

"I don't usually do feet metaphorically." When the scarf was undone he used it, one end in each hand, to draw her to him. "I like to do lips."

Morgan had no thought of avoiding his kiss, but the greediness of it surprised her. He opened his mouth over hers and tasted her with a fiery need. She reached for him instinctively, arms winding around his neck, inhaling the scent of his hair. She grew warm, and her pulse shifted into fast-dance gear; the scarf tightened at the back of her neck as his thumbs caressed her jaw and he slanted his mouth to demand her response from a different angle.

Long-buried need welled up in him. Here was a woman he wanted to give to, and when he had given, he would want to give more. He would take her hair down again and make her comfortable with her femininity, make her feel how beautiful she was. Breathless, he laid his forehead against hers and whispered the word. "Beautiful."

"Like what?" she asked, her eyes still closed.

"Fruit ripening in the warm summer sun."

"What kind?"

He tasted again, sipping gently this time, touching her lower lip with the tip of his tongue. "Peaches," he decided. "Sweet. My favorite."

"I would have said raspberries for you," she whispered, and brushed her lips against his. "Tangy. *My* favorite."

"We should have lunch sometime." He returned her soft kiss, then planted another on her chin.

"We're not in season."

"That might be what makes us taste so good to each other. It's been a while since summer."

The truth of his statement hit her hard. He rose above her, another kiss in his eyes, and she drew back. She'd had her summer with a charming dreamer, and she knew it was a short season. "That's true," she said. "It's been a long time."

"Did the metaphor go sour?"

"No." She smiled, not completely uncomfortable with the effectiveness of his charm. "It's lovely, and I'm flattered."

"You're more than flattered," he said quietly.

She nodded and allowed herself an unsteady sigh. "I'm more than flattered. That's how I know it's time for me to go home. We can dress up and pretend for a while but, let's face it, we're not two teenagers necking on the sofa."

"Uh-uh. We're not."

She moved back on the seat, and his arm slid away from her. "Which means games are not in order. It's either friends or lovers."

"Why not both?"

"Because it wouldn't work." She rose to her feet as though convinced, but somewhere in the back of her mind she knew she wasn't. There was an obstinate part of her that didn't want to be. "I like being friends with you, though. You're a good dancer and a fantastic cook."

Mikal settled back on the sofa, giving her a slow, self-satisfied grin. "And you're still nervous. You're even a little scared."

"Maybe that's the only smart way for me to be. Thanks for the evening." She gave him an apologetic smile and turned toward the door. "Good night, Mikal."

"Good night," he called after her as the door closed behind her. He stared at the coffee she'd left behind and listened to the roar of her car engine as she fed it too much gas. "If you were so smart, Morgan Kramer, you'd realize there's only one thing that won't work with us. And that, my lady, is *just* being friends."

## Chapter Five

*Can I love someone else after loving you?*

He'd thought it might be the beginning of something when he'd first written the line, but all it did was repeat itself, both in his mind and on the paper. Many of his poems were questions that required no answers, but this wasn't one of those. This question definitely needed an answer.

Mikal rarely discussed his wife anymore, except when David asked about her. The memories were all good ones now, and the pain was little more than a dull ache. He hadn't led a celibate life in the ten years since her death, but he'd loved no other woman. He told himself there'd been no time for that. Sharon was still with him in so many ways that he'd been able to convince himself that nothing was really missing. He was a passionate man, but he had many outlets for his passion. His writing was a testimony to that. And his life was filled with love—love for his son, for those who worked with him and shared his beliefs, for Peg and for Yuri. He hadn't been looking for a close relationship with a woman.

Now there was Morgan. So many pictures of her came to his mind at once. There was the school principal, dressed for business, letting him know that she was concerned about his son, but that she would tolerate no more of the boy's nonsense. Then there was the exercise instructor, dressed in a leotard and convincing a gym full of preteens that working up a sweat was truly fun. Mikal smiled to himself as he remembered Morgan's story and pictured the prim and studious lady finding she'd finally built a muscle and secretly crowing at the accomplishment.

She'd come to his house as the proper dinner guest, but she'd willingly put on an apron and started cooking. She'd gone to a rally with the intention of listening to what he had to say, and she'd accepted a role in that, too. She was more flexible than she realized. He'd turned her classic outfit into a fifties costume, and she'd taken the cue, nearly dancing him under the table. And on the hill above the Missouri River, with the morning sky painting streaks all around them, she'd let him take her hair down. *That* was the image he treasured. That was the one haunting him day and night. He'd made it happen again after the dance, and he remembered how she'd looked then—relaxed, her hazel eyes soft and sleepy. She'd let her hair fall loosely around her shoulders, and her mouth had been berry-stained with the remnants of "Cherries in the Snow." She'd lifted her face to him, and he could still taste that kiss.

Mikal needed a good swift kick in the pants. His typewriter hummed, and the words, "Can I love someone else after loving you?" stared up at him. With an audible growl, he ripped the paper from the machine, wadded it in his fist and pitched it toward the wastepaper basket.

"Of course I can," he told the typewriter as though it had posed the question. "If I want to love somebody, I'll love somebody. Just as soon as I have the time. I have a book to finish first, and I have to..."

He tapped his fingers lightly against the keys, not typing, just thinking. He was well into the middle of this book. He knew when his work was good, and this was. *A Free Country* was better than *The Last Barnraising*. It was a refugee's story. The main character was a composite of a number of people he'd come to know through his work with Freedom International, people whom Uncle Yuri called "freedom seekers." Mikal knew that this would be an important book, that it was timely, and that Americans were ready to read it. He just had to write it.

He heard the phone ring, and he pushed his chair back, mumbling an expression he wouldn't want his son to hear him use. Apparently David had picked up the phone, though, so maybe he *had* heard it. When Mikal wasn't called within a few seconds, he rolled his chair back under his desk and set his fingers on the typewriter keys again. If he weren't so damned disorganized, he thought, he'd get more done.

Get organized, then, he told himself. You have so many hours for writing, so many for David, so many for consciousness-raising, and if you want to see Morgan, you have to plan for that, too. Right now, you're writing. Mikal tilted his head back and laughed at his own delusion. Above his desk was a bulletin board with notes to himself, some of them a year old. He'd tried. He'd had this conversation with himself before. David had given him an appointment book, which he'd never used. It was full of square blocks of time, and Mikal couldn't fit the flow of his life into square blocks of time. *Always* there was David, and *always* his writing, and *always* the things he believed in.

And now, too, there was Morgan. God help him, she was not going to go away. In fact, he didn't want her to. With that settled in his mind, Mikal began pecking at the typewriter.

David waited until suppertime to tell his father about the phone call. He knew he'd be in trouble. Phone calls from Uncle Yuri were not to be considered interruptions. Without looking up from his plate of eggplant made so even a kid could love it, David said, "Uncle Yuri called today."

"Uncle Yuri?" Mikal laid his fork back on his plate. "Where was I?"

"You were in the office."

"Why didn't you tell me he was on the phone? Didn't he ask for me?"

"Well, yeah," David admitted with a shrug. "I told him you were busy writing. He just wants to know if you're going to Philadelphia."

Pulling the napkin up from his lap, Mikal sighed and wiped his chin. "That fancy affair is for the national office and big-money contributors. They don't need me for that kind of stuff. I'm satisfied to do my bit at the local level. I'm no good at—"

"He says you are." Mikal gave David a helpless look, as if hoping somebody would sympathize with him. "I'm sorry, Dad, but he says they need you. That was the message."

Mikal knew what Yuri had in mind for him, and he knew that in the end he wouldn't refuse. Mikal would get the commitments. He had the knack for it. "It's over the Thanksgiving holiday, and I hate to be away from home then."

David drew lines in the melted Parmesan cheese with his fork. He knew his father played an important role in the organization's work, but he suspected there was more to this work than he'd been privy to. There'd been times when he'd had an uneasy feeling about Mikal's trips. "You don't think they need you for anything . . . special this time, do you?"

"Special?" Mikal watched as David played with his food.

"Overseas or something." Looking up at his father, David added quickly, "Like one of those investigations, or whatever they are."

"No, this is just a fund-raiser. You have to go around glad-handing everybody and being very..." With a sigh, Mikal admitted, "But it has to be done, and I guess I can do my share."

"You're never gonna finish that book, Dad."

"Of course I will." Mikal sipped his coffee and regarded his son thoughtfully. He hadn't discussed the full implications of his work with Freedom International because he'd always thought David was too young to understand and that he might worry unnecessarily. The next time "something special" came up, David had a right to know, Mikal decided. But this time it *was* just a fund-raiser.

"You know what I was thinking?" Mikal began, and David looked up, curious. "I was thinking of asking Miss Kramer to go with me."

"Take Miss Kramer?" From the look on David's face, Mikal might have suggested that they have something wonderful for dessert. "To Philadelphia?" Mikal nodded. "You think she'd go?"

"Why not?" A picture formed in Mikal's mind of the two of them bounding up the steps of the Philadelphia Museum of Art together. He liked what he saw.

"Yeah, why not?" David smiled as he pictured the look on Miss Kramer's face when she got a load of Mikal Romanov in a tux. His dad was one cool-looking dude when he got dressed up. "I don't think she's ever been to Philadelphia. And now that you've got her interested in Freedom International..." If Miss Kramer were going on this trip, it couldn't be one of those special assignments, David told himself. "I think she'd go for it, Dad."

Mikal grinned, thinking of the art museum steps again. "So do I."

Morgan watched the airplane's wing cut through the white mist of clouds as it dipped in its final approach to the runway below. She felt her stomach flutter and wasn't sure whether to blame it on a bump in the air or the knot in her nerves. In truth it was probably neither. Her stomach had been fluttering from the first moment Mikal had suggested this trip. She'd known from the start that the whole idea had been blown through a dreamer's pipe and that she had no business climbing into his bubble and drifting off with him. She'd also known she would go.

She hadn't agreed right away, not because she was playing coy, but because her brain had insisted she give voice to a list of reasonable objections. All the while her heart had been playing jump rope in her chest. Mikal must have seen her answer in her eyes when he first offered his proposal, but he listened to all her excuses. When she ran out, he concluded, "You'll go, then?"

"You're really serious, aren't you?"

"Of course I'm serious. I want to take you to Philadelphia with me. Otherwise I don't want to go."

"But this is your job, sort of.... Isn't it?"

He laughed. "I don't have a job. I have a mission. I have—" he waved his hand near his temple "—a vision." She rolled her eyes and thought, *Don't remind me.* "I see the two of us running up the steps of the art museum, you in your leotard, me in my gray sweats."

"Dream on, Mr. Romanov."

He did. "I see us having dinner at a little place I know on South Street. Flowers. Candlelight. Soft music." By that time she was smiling and her heart was skipping double-dutch, which he must have sensed because he added, "An old-fashioned date, Morgan. My treat."

Now Morgan rolled her head against the high-backed seat and looked over at Mikal, who'd slept through most of the flight from Minneapolis. He'd refused the airline lunch, though Morgan had found it passable, and mumbling an apology for being poor company, he'd fallen asleep. He'd been at the type-writer most of the night, and it occurred to Morgan that for a man who didn't have a job, Mikal worked very hard. Now he slept hard, undisturbed by the change of pressure caused by the plane's descent. His chin rested on his chest as he listed toward Morgan. She thought that if she moved a little closer, his head might drop to her shoulder and he might be more comfortable. It was a whimsical urge, she told herself firmly, probably brought on by the fact that he looked almost childlike as he slept. His thick, yellow-brown hair was tumbling over his forehead, and his full lips were parted just slightly. She noticed the plush length of his eyelashes for the first time.

The plane touched down, and Mikal sat up, stretching and shaking off sleep like a lion awakening from an afternoon nap. He was, Morgan realized, the epitome of the natural man, which was probably at the root of his charm. Comfortable with himself, he put others at ease. He smiled at her, and she felt herself melt.

"I'm glad you came," he assured her, covering her hand with his. Morgan felt uneasy, as if all the sound and speed of the airplane were crowding into the pit of her stomach. "I've been anxious for you to meet Uncle Yuri, but don't let him rattle you. He's direct, impatient and dictatorial, but his insides are made of chocolate mousse."

"That sweet?"

"And that soft." Mikal grinned at the thought. "He's going to love you."

Yuri Romanov paused on his way down the concourse to check the computer screen for the gate number. With a glance at his watch, he proceeded at a pace that proudly denied any question of physical deterioration, even though he was seventy-four. There was no time in his day for stiff joints or aching muscles. He was always busy, always moving with deliberation and purpose, as he did now to await the arrival of his nephew and the woman he would bring, presumably for Yuri's approval. Yuri was anxious to see them both, and he was annoyed by the flight's delay. When Mikal's face appeared above the crowd of passengers who were streaming into the terminal, annoyance was forgotten. The old man's heart swelled with pride.

The garment bag Mikal had slung over his shoulder slipped to the floor as he reached for his uncle Yuri. Morgan snatched up the bag and draped it over the back of a chair as she watched the two big men greet each other with unreserved bear hugs, the older man bussing the younger on both cheeks. Uncle Yuri was the image of the man Mikal would be in another thirty-five years. Yuri was heavier, but his eyes were just as blue, and he had a full head of thick, white hair the same texture as Mikal's.

"Uncle Yuri, this is my friend, Morgan Kramer."

Yuri took the hand Morgan offered, but he brushed his lips over the back of it. "You're lovely, my dear, and I'm delighted." He turned to Mikal. "How good a friend?"

Mikal laughed as he retrieved Morgan's bag. "A very good friend, Uncle Yuri."

Yuri's embrace took Morgan by surprise, and her eyes widened. "A *good* friend! Welcome, welcome, dear lady. Mikal sometimes brings his friends to see me, but always they are friends of the cause first, *then* friends of Mikal's." His smile was meant to reassure her as he surrounded her shoulders with one arm and squeezed. "You will have a fascinating and enjoyable holiday, and I promise to see that Mikal has plenty of time to spend with you."

His smile was as irresistible as his nephew's. It melted the stiffness from her shoulders as she stood pinned under his arm. "I've been looking forward to meeting you, Mr. Romanov. Mikal talks about you a great deal."

"All good, Uncle Yuri, except that whenever there's a woman around, she ends up on your arm while I carry the bags." Mikal was holding two of Morgan's and one of his own. "Morgan refused to check hers through, but I'll have to pick up one of mine at the baggage claim area."

"Very wise, my dear," Yuri said, settling Morgan's hand in the crook of his elbow. "I always refuse to let them lose mine. It can ruin a holiday when your baggage is delayed."

"If they lose my tux, I'll just have to wear something else." Mikal fell into step with Yuri and Morgan, shouldering his way past a flock of teenagers who'd just spotted someone whose arrival touched off peals of excitement.

Yuri shot Mikal a fatherly glance. "If they lose your tux, we'll get you another one."

"My poetry is more convincing if I'm allowed to read it looking the part of the poet."

"I have much more in mind for you than the reading of poetry. Do you think I would allow you to get up in front of our benefactors in blue jeans and a sweatshirt?" Yuri glanced down at Morgan and reassured them both. "He knows his job well, but he thinks it's fun to rile an old man. His grandmother would never have allowed him to appear in public without a tie, not even in Bismarck."

Morgan detected a note of disdain in the way he enunciated the last word. "Mikal's poetry sounds beautiful no matter how he's dressed."

Yuri's eyes brightened and crinkled at the corners as he gave his nephew an approving smile. She was just the kind of woman Mikal needed—warm, wise and patient. One who would give his ego the boost it needed, but not object to the time he had to spend on his work. And Mikal was needed; Yuri had work for him to do.

"You have a treasure here, Mikal. Keep her happy. I trust you turned your nose up at airline food. The hotel has excellent dining facilities. I'll see that the baggage is taken to your rooms. How was your weather in Bismarck?"

Mikal knew that North Dakota had never been Yuri's favorite place. He'd tried many times to persuade Mikal to move to the east coast, where he'd be closer to the daily business of the organization. "Great," Mikal reported. "Crisp, clean fall weather. Brisk."

Yuri laughed. "Euphemisms. I know North Dakota, dear children. I grew up there. November can be a monster, and the snow and wind can continue into May." It reminded him of Russia and the bitterly cold trip he had taken long ago to leave there. He'd been terrified at the time because his father, always a man of such courage, had been afraid of something too awful to name. Years later, when Yuri had left the Midwest for college in the east, he'd never called it home again, and he'd never missed the prairie's icy winter blasts. Its one point of interest for him was Mikal, and he couldn't understand why his nephew made his home there.

"Not this year," Mikal said, hoping to dismiss his uncle's usual indictment of North Dakota. "The weather's been fine."

Morgan took a mental backseat as she sat close to Mikal in the cab and watched the sights of the city pass by the window. While the men talked of the upcoming event, she absorbed the contrasts between the city she'd left and the one she was visiting. They were the same kind of contrasts she was beginning to sense between Mikal and his uncle—the private man who took life as it came, quietly making it fit his terms, and the man who represented an international movement, met the world with a list of demands, made noise and made news. For every urgency of Yuri's there was a quiet response from Mikal. Morgan wondered how they got along as well as they seemed to.

At the hotel the bellman took the bags as Mikal and Yuri went to the desk. "You did reserve two rooms as I asked." Mikal knew his uncle well.

"Of course, Mikal. Do you take me for a boor? I respect a lady's privacy. You have two separate rooms." He clapped a hand on Mikal's shoulder and tossed him a wink. "Adjoining, of course. She is lovely, my boy."

"It's just as I told you," Mikal said, smiling as Morgan turned from the display of paintings she'd stopped to examine. Her loveliness was a fact to which he took no exception. She was living proof that the dark-haired, fair-skinned beauty in the painting behind her could have been a reality. "She's a very good friend."

"I can see that, and I approve." Yuri gave his nephew another reassuring pat on the shoulder. "Have dinner with your good friend now. Tonight you'll have a drink with Marshal Kost and tomorrow lunch with—" he drew his notes from his breast pocket to refresh his memory "—Stan Levine. Miss Kramer would be an asset in your meeting with Levine, but not Kost. Kost is a man of purpose, and he resents distractions."

Mikal understood his uncle. Nothing in Yuri's life had ever interfered with his work. Each time they met, Mikal had to set Yuri straight on his own priorities. "Yuri, listen to me. Morgan is not here to be an asset. She's a guest. I intend to see that she enjoys herself." He crooked a finger at Yuri's notes. "Just hand over the appointments and let me deal with them."

Joining them near the desk, Morgan glanced at the paper. They were two men who shared strong beliefs, cared for one another, worked together, but whose styles were totally different. Two different sources of power. Two hands on an apparently important list.

Mikal waited for the list of appointments. "You do trust me to do my job?" he asked quietly.

Yes, Yuri thought, I've always trusted you, but you've never brought a woman along before. How will she change you? How *has* she changed you? To another man, the idea of a woman as an asset would not be offensive, but to Mikal... Yuri should have known better. "You've done well for us in this role. I would allow no one else to deal with these people."

"Nothing's changed. I know what our needs are and I know how to meet them." Yuri relinquished the list, and Mikal pocketed it with a smile. "Your ways might be as good as mine, Uncle Yuri, but they're different. We're not the same man."

The concern disappeared from Yuri's face as he laughed. "I'm too old to be the man you are. And I never had your charm, even when I might have had some of your patience. Do it your way, Mikal. It always works."

## Chapter Six

Morgan liked taking her things out of a suitcase and arranging them in an orderly fashion, ready to be used. She liked having places for things, particularly herself. The fact that her room adjoined Mikal's didn't bother her. She had her own bed and her own place to unwind. Knowing that he was in the next room gave her a good feeling, because the rest of the scene promised to be foreign to her. She had attended conferences before, mostly for educators, but they had never been glamorous or high-pressure, which was what she expected from an organization courting big money. She knew she could count on Mikal to be a breath of unaffected midwestern air.

Mikal's knock came at the hallway door, not at the one between their rooms. She opened the door to find him standing there dressed in a trim, blue suit. What surprised her was not the suit itself, though she'd never seen him wear one, but the fact that he looked as comfortable in it as he did in his customary pullover. His tawny, slightly coarse hair fell into place naturally. Morgan remembered the way he'd joined her exercise class, the way he'd read his poetry for the Bismarck group, the way he'd looked when he was made up for the oldies dance. No matter how he dressed or what he did, he was always comfortable with his role. He was always Mikal. He adjusted the knot in his tie and grinned, blue eyes flashing. "Didn't think I owned one, did you?"

"I like it. It matches your eyes."

"That's what the saleswoman told me. She said I was a real knockout in this suit. Are you reeling?"

She was, but she couldn't manage a direct admission. "I'm suit-ably impressed." With a groan, he offered his arm. "Wasn't that good highbrow humor?" she teased.

"Classy as hell, Miss Kramer. You're seated at my table for the duration, no matter what Uncle Yuri says. I can use a laugh once in a while."

The table they shared for dinner was tucked in a private corner in a dimly lit dining room. The decor was so plush and the voices so hushed that Morgan felt as though she'd been wrapped in velvet. Mikal discouraged her first choice, which was steak, and suggested rack of lamb or poached salmon. She ordered stuffed fillet of beef and challenged him with an arched eyebrow. With a shrug, he opted for the fish.

"What do you think of Uncle Yuri?" Mikal asked, bracing himself both physically and mentally as he planted his elbows at the edge of the table and laced his fingers together.

"It's too early to tell," Morgan replied. "I'm still wondering what he thinks of me. I take it 'good friend' is another euphemism."

"Uncle Yuri has never been married. He contends that he can't commit himself to a marriage because of his commitment to Freedom International." Mikal considered the candle in the center of the table for a moment. "I've told him that's garbage. He's loved the same woman for twenty years, and he should have married her a long time ago. Helen's a fine lady." He lifted his gaze to Morgan's face. "I guess it's their business."

"Maybe it's best. If he's not a family man, at least he never pretended to be."

He noted the dignified way she held her chin up, shoulders squared. She wasn't thinking about Uncle Yuri. "People make lots of commitments in the course of a lifetime, and one doesn't necessarily cancel out all the others. Your mother made some choices, too."

"Yes, but my father..." She saw him in her mind and the image worked on her as it always did. She missed him. "They did stay married, though I've never understood why. When my mother died, my father truly became a widower."

"Uncle Yuri is committed to Helen in his way, too. She knows who he is, what he is, and she's always accepted that. When he dies, she'll be a widow, whether he marries her or not. He needs to recognize that."

"Maybe having a 'good friend' is the best he can do," Morgan suggested.

"Maybe."

"Maybe he thinks every man should have at least one 'good friend.'" She was teasing now, a smile sneaking into her eyes.

"I agree, but then 'good friend' isn't a euphemism to me. You have to take Uncle Yuri with a grain of salt. He thinks he's grooming me for something, and I think I'm pretty well groomed as it is." He ran a thumb under his lapel and adjusted his tie. "What do you think?"

"I think you're a knockout."

After dinner Morgan and Mikal strolled through the hotel's huge, glass-walled lobby, with its arching escalators and profusion of lush greenery. They window-shopped in the hotel's mall, admiring the displays in the exclusive stores. When the time came for Mikal's appointment, Morgan half hoped he'd skip it. He asked her to join him, but she professed a need for sleep before she could manage more sociability. He walked her back to her room and lingered at the door for a time, letting them both enjoy the bittersweet regret that went with their long, slow kiss and whispered good-nights.

\* \* \*

At breakfast Morgan watched the Romanov charm go to work. She lost count of the number of people Mikal greeted. No name escaped him, and he showed a genuine interest in some aspect of each person's life when he asked about families and businesses and listened attentively to the answers. When they left the dining room, Morgan noticed that most of Mikal's meal was still on his plate.

Morgan listened to speakers during the rest of the morning, while Mikal seemed to come and go from the meeting rooms. He moved with the casual assurance of one who commanded respect and attention, though he made no demands. Nothing appeared to push him, and he never pushed. He always had an easy smile for Morgan, a comment or two about the speaker, and a way of touching her arm that suggested a special intimacy.

As Yuri had promised, they had lunch with Stan Levine, a man who enjoyed being distracted from his nervous stomach by beautiful young women. He spoke with a trace of an East European accent, and his age was hard to guess. His face had probably never looked young. Morgan accepted his barrage of compliments graciously. Mikal suffered them briefly, then turned the conversation to food.

"You kids order whatever you like," Stan said, scanning the menu with a face that looked predisposed to be disgusted. "Nothing agrees with me. There's nothing on here I can eat."

"You're sadly in need of a dietician, Stan." Mikal looked the menu over quickly.

"Oh, I've gone that route. No point in eating if the food's tasteless."

"Let me try something out on you." Mikal wrote a note to the kitchen and gave it to the waiter, along with his order and Morgan's. "If this gives you any problem, let me know. I'll be honor-bound to find a remedy."

Stan's lunch consisted of a clear soup and a chicken dish that Stan pronounced delicious. "But, you know, I can't have salt," he cautioned after the second bite.

Mikal smiled. "There isn't any."

"Mmm." Stan studied the next forkful of food as if still searching for some sign of salt, which he apparently didn't find. "Tasty. I'll take the recipe."

"I have several others," Mikal said. "Use them in good health."

"My mother would bless you for that, though she'd be surprised to find a man who could cook as well as she does." There was a faraway sadness in the older man's eyes that tugged at Morgan's heart.

"I understand you've had no contact with your mother since you came to this country," Mikal said. "How long has it been?"

"Thirty years." Stan's deep sigh seemed to pull him backward through those years, one at a time. "I've tried government agencies, the Red Cross, and I get nothing. I'm told she died, but I'm denied proof. I'm told she moved. I'm told she never existed. Never existed! I'm here, right? Therefore she existed."

"Of course," Mikal said quietly, his voice a balm even for Morgan, who suffered vicariously as she witnessed Stan Levine's anguish. "You're feeling cut off at the roots. Whether she's alive or dead, you need to know."

"I believe she was imprisoned." Stan stabbed at his food. "I'm sure of it."

"Have you been in touch with any of her friends?"

Stan shook his head, despairing, "It's so difficult to get answers out of them. Double-talk, secrets, cover-ups. I can't tell you how discouraging it is."

"Yes you can. And I can believe every word," Mikal assured him, and the man's tired eyes filled with gratitude.

"My wife tells me to give up, but I can't give up. My mother helped me escape. She had a good job, a little influence." He shrugged. "She risked it all, used it all to help me. Now I want you to help me find her." His demand became a plea. "At least help me find the truth."

Mikal laid a comforting hand on the man's forearm. "Give us all the information you have."

"Make her a high priority. Please. My contribution will be—"

Mikal waved the promise away. "Because of your mother's age, I think this will be seen as an urgent case. We need contributions, but they have nothing to do with the way our investigations are handled. You can give anonymously, and I guarantee we will be looking for your mother within a month."

Morgan felt Stan's relief. Mikal's manner was as soothing to his anxious mind as his food was to the poor man's sensitive stomach. "How good was your promise?" she asked Mikal after they'd left Stan with handshakes and good wishes.

"As good as gold. He should've come to us sooner, though. It's hard to cut through thirty years."

"It really doesn't matter how much money he can contribute?"

Mikal slipped an arm around her shoulders as they walked through the sunlit lobby. "It really doesn't matter. Donations and investigations are handled completely separately."

"But your uncle must have his hands in both pies." His frown told her she'd chosen the wrong words. "Figuratively, of course."

"His concern with both aspects of the organization is literal, though. We're audited regularly. Our overhead is consistently low in comparison with that of other charitable organizations. And what we do is vitally important, Morgan." She looked up at him, and he knew she was willing to believe him. "We keep the world's eyes open."

The same message resounded throughout the afternoon presentations. Human beings must not be put away and forgotten. Morgan recalled Mr. Levine's anguish and began to feel deeply that this was true. She listened to stories like his, each one demanding its own attention, its own personal responses. Conditions, policies and politics were discussed, questioned, even roundly debated by speakers and their audiences, but at the heart of the matter for Morgan was Mr. Levine's mother.

"We have a couple of hours before we'll have to get dolled up for tonight's banquet. How about a walk over to the park?" Mikal offered, catching up with her as she emerged from a meeting room. "You must be tired of sitting."

"I am." Hands at her waist, Morgan stretched her back and rolled her shoulders. "I'm not tired of listening, though. That doctor who lived in Swaziland was just fascinating."

He put his hand around her elbow and slid it along her silken sleeve to press his palm against hers. "I'm just fascinating, too," he muttered near her ear. "You want card tricks or kisses?"

"While we're walking?"

"All three at once, if you like." He squeezed her hand and gave her a wink. "That's what makes me so fascinating."

"Mikal, may I have a word with you?"

They stopped and waited for Yuri. He was accompanied by a shorter man dressed in a conservative gray suit. Morgan felt Mikal's body stiffen before he released her hand. She glanced up and watched him force himself to relax and accept the shorter man's handshake. "Alex," he acknowledged.

"It's good to have you back, Mikal."

"Only for the fund-raiser, Alex. Nothing more." Morgan felt the strange current of emotion between the two men as Mikal turned to draw her into the conversation. It wasn't really outright antagonism; it was more a mutual defensiveness. "Morgan, this is Alex Steiger, a member of the board of directors. Alex, Morgan Kramer."

Morgan extended her hand, and Alex greeted her cordially, but he was clearly not a man to linger on the social amenities. "If I might have a few moments with you, Mikal, there are a few matters—"

"We were just going for a walk. Perhaps tomorrow," Mikal suggested.

"I have to be in Washington tomorrow morning. I'm not going to ask you to negotiate any treaties, Mikal." Alex glanced at Yuri for confirmation, which he gave with a nod. "Your uncle feels that we should visit with each other about some—" he waved his hand in a dismissive gesture "—organizational business while you're here. I've asked a couple of the members of the board to join us."

"And I would like nothing better than to take a walk this evening," Yuri put in. "If you can keep up with me, Morgan. I tend to worry that my time is short, and I forget to take it easy."

Morgan looked at Mikal and felt a stab of disappointment when he nodded. He was more than the "glad-hander" for the organization that he'd claimed to be, and the meeting with Alex Steiger was to be more than a casual discussion. Mikal was being drawn away from her, and she didn't like the feeling that left her with. Lifting her chin, she beat the sensation down. "I think I can manage," Morgan said, accepting Yuri's proffered arm. "We'll take periodic pulse checks. I'll be ready by eight, Mikal."

There was something singularly stylish about the way Yuri strolled down the street with Morgan on his arm. It was like finding a man who was truly a good dancer. Morgan felt her spirits lifting and her heart warming to the man simply because the evening was balmy and the smooth, unhurried motion felt so fine.

"What's the problem between Mikal and Alex?" Morgan asked as they waited for the light at a corner.

"You're very perceptive," Yuri said without looking down at her.

"It was impossible to miss the tension there. Mikal is *never* like that."

"'Mikal is *never* like that'?" Yuri echoed with a smile. "How long have you known him?"

"Long enough," popped into Morgan's mind, much to her own surprise, but the light changed and she decided the question didn't warrant an answer.

"It doesn't matter," Yuri said, dismissing his own presumptuousness. "You'll know him as long as I have and still continue to see new beauty in him. Alex is an attorney, our specialist in international law, and a brilliant man, but he knows it's Mikal who's the heir apparent."

"Heir to whom?"

He gave her a look of patient disbelief. "To me. But, of course, Mikal resists. A grass roots man, he calls himself." With a short laugh he added, "It sounds like a group from the early sixties. Mikal Romanov, the grass roots man. Absurd!"

"Mikal is a writer," Morgan reminded him.

"He is a man who is acutely aware of everything that goes on around him. That awareness forces him to speak out in many ways. What's more important, though, is his gift for touching the heart of the matter without flourish or fanfare. He reaches people."

"So you want him to do more work for Freedom International, and that's what Alex has been assigned to talk with him about."

"Alex takes this upon himself," Yuri explained. "There are times when Mikal's talents are invaluable."

"He's here for your fund-raiser, and he's certainly reaching people. I'd say you're getting your money's worth out of him."

They had come to the edge of a park and slowed to turn around and head back. Yuri paused to make his point. "Mikal is not paid for what he does for us right now. We use his name and pay his expenses to bring him here, because, as I said, he reaches people. We want him to do more. We want him to negotiate for us on a regular basis."

"Negotiate...prisoner releases and things like that?"

"We do a great deal of negotiating for releases, improved conditions for prisoners, and so on. Sometimes in a hostage situation we'll be called in, discreetly, of course. Governments are supposed to take care of these things."

Resuming the walk, Morgan considered the pavement under her feet. "Apparently, Mikal has some choices to make."

"We have used him on a couple of occasions in the past, and he is a master. A situation is developing now that we've been unofficially invited to look into. Alex is talking to Mikal about serving on the team."

"Obviously it isn't the kind of thing Mikal wants to do."

"We understand his reasons. Mikal has a son to think about. But it is the kind of thing he does extremely well, and, as you say, he has some choices to make."

Morgan chose not to ask whether it was the kind of thing that might also be extremely dangerous. In the movies the enemy usually made an example of the guy who carried the white flag.

Mikal carried a red rose. When he appeared at her door a few minutes before eight Morgan allowed herself a moment just to admire him. His black tuxedo was cut to accentuate his broad shoulders and long torso. His pleated shirtfront was ivory, which was particularly flattering to the golden tone of his skin. She stepped back, not to escape, but to draw him over the threshold.

Mikal followed, closing the door behind him. Morgan's long, sleek, red dress was stunning and very provocative in the way it moved over her slender body with silken fluidity. Her hair was caught up off her neck, leaving a long column of soft, translucent skin that he would have to touch before he could decide whether it was real or not. Wordlessly he put the long-stemmed rose in her hand and drew her into his arms, his mouth descending to give her something more. She offered no resistance. Her arms went around his neck as she lifted her body to his embrace, melted into it, then returned his gift with one of her own. With a guttural groan, he tightened his arms around her and deepened his kiss.

Their mingling breaths quickened as the kiss, given and returned, grew hot and urgent. Mikal's hands moved in slow circles over Morgan's back. The silky fabric of her dress moved with him, and he learned exactly what she wore underneath it. With his mouth he tested the softness of her neck and the sleekness of her jawline while he nuzzled the heady scent behind her ear.

"I could easily do without this banquet business," he whispered, keeping his mouth where it was.

The heat of his breath made Morgan shiver. "But we're all dressed."

"I could easily do without that, too."

"I thought you'd like this dress."

"I love it." His hand slid over her bottom as he tightened his hold. "Oh, God, I love it."

He held her against him, pillowing his hard length against the soft pliancy of her body, and she sucked in a breath, inhaling the sweet scent of the rose. "Mmm, so good," Morgan whispered.

Mikal heard music in Morgan's soft voice. Tenderly he kissed the mouth that made it. "Let's lock the door and take the phone off the hook."

Morgan brushed her fingers through the hair over his temple, and Mikal detected a hint of sadness in her smile. "I'm afraid that wouldn't take *you* off the hook."

"How can anyone so beautiful be so sensible?"

"It's not such an odd combination—" she gave him a saucy smile as she let her hand slide down his satin lapel "—in a *woman*. Incidentally you're beautiful tonight, too."

"Men aren't beautiful."

She touched his black bow tie and ran her thumbnail along a pleat in his shirt. "In the eyes of this beholder you are."

"But not sensible?"

"Dreamers don't have to be. You did say there'd be dancing after dinner?" Mikal nodded, knowing that eating a predictable banquet dinner of chicken à la king was an inevitability now. "How many contributors will you have to dance with?"

"None. I have a date."

Mikal found the chicken Kiev to be a pleasant surprise, but he ate little of it before giving his poetry reading. The crowd was moved, some to tears, and Morgan knew that he touched a chord of loss for many of them. She saw, too, that whereas at home he was the town's eccentric, here he was revered as an artist and a visionary. Watching him and listening, she remembered seeing her father surrounded by people who took his message to heart, and she felt the swelling in her own breast. She had always loved her father, and now she loved another who was just like him. There was no help for it.

Mikal kept his promise and danced with Morgan to the exclusion of all others. Surrounded by music and mirrors and chandeliers, both were too absorbed to notice another living soul. They moved over the polished floor with the grace of unconscious effort, seeing only each other. Morgan had imagined herself in such a place with such a man many times, and now she glided, light-headed from dreams rather than drinks, and enamored with Mikal's beauty.

Stan Levine joined Yuri at the bar and tipped a glass toward the waltzing couple. "I'd hoped for a dance with her," he said, "but there's a special aura about them. I couldn't cut in."

Yuri nodded, sipping his Scotch. "I'm having the same trouble."

It was later, after the last waltz had been played, that Yuri joined the two for a drink beside the pool. They sat in chairs with canvas-covered cushions and talked in the hushed tones befitting the late hour. Lights at the bottom of the pool cast purling shadows on the ceiling, and Morgan could almost feel the water's warm caress.

"Where's Helen, Uncle Yuri? It's unlike her to miss the fall fund-raiser."

Smiling at his nephew, Yuri translated the message into his own terms. Mikal's lady was at his side, and he wished the same joy for the rest of the world's male population. In a few minutes, he thought, I'll leave you alone with her. "She's with her sister in Utica. Doris hasn't been well, so Helen spends more time with her. She sends you her best." He settled back in his chair and studied Mikal for a moment. "Alex tells me you aren't interested in being included on this mission."

"The whole thing sounds pretty iffy," Mikal said. "*If* there's actually been a coup, and *if* there are actually hostages, and *if* whoever's in charge will see me. We don't even know who we'd be dealing with." He offered Morgan an explanation. "It's one of those overnight revolutions, with everything still up in the air as far as who's taken over whom. There may be American hostages."

"I haven't heard anything in the news about a revolution," Morgan said.

"It hasn't been called that yet," Mikal answered. "As I said, it's all very iffy, and it isn't my bailiwick. Let Alex handle it."

"Alex is excellent when it comes to facts, figures and codes of law, but he's no good one-on-one, Mikal. You are. You must not withhold your talents when they're so desperately needed. If our information is correct, we may be able to get these people out before the media calls them hostages and forces the new government to put on a show of strength."

Mikal watched the reflections from the water dance above his head. He spoke quietly. "We all have choices to make, Uncle Yuri. I make mine much more carefully than I used to. My book is going well, and I want to finish it, and then I want to start another one. If I do this now, within a matter of weeks or months there'll be another mission. You take care of the politics, Uncle Yuri, you and Alex."

Yuri turned to Morgan, looking for help. After all, didn't every woman hope her man would rise to greatness? "The world would thank you if you would talk some sense into this man, my dear."

Morgan looked at Mikal and saw his fatigue, familiar not because she'd seen it in his eyes before but from memories of her father. It occurred to her that it was not the work that brought this kind of weariness but the unending demands, the knowledge that meeting one need only left a thousand more. "You were right about choices, Mikal. My father made his, my mother hers. And yours are no easier to make."

His appreciative smile made her pulse flutter. Without taking his eyes from her, he explained to his uncle, "We've decided you should meet Morgan's father, Uncle Yuri. He's a missionary. In fact, maybe we could all pay him a visit. I could use a Caribbean holiday along about January." He hastened to add, "A real holiday, with no strings attached."

"Is your father in the Bahamas or one of the American islands?" Yuri asked, interested.

"Further south," Morgan told him. "A little to the west of Cuba. One of those little banana republics."

"De Colores?"

"Yes." The glance Yuri exchanged with Mikal puzzled her. "Have you been there?" she wondered.

"Uh, yes," Yuri answered. "Yes, I have. Years ago. Lovely island." He laid a hand on Mikal's forearm as he moved to the edge of his chair, preparing to stand. "We've very little information on this other thing,

Mikal. Nothing official. I'm sure you'll want to be kept informed."

Mikal's brow was pulled into a deep frown. "You'll be making more inquiries?"

"We're doing that now. The entire report may be unfounded, and there may be no need for our...services. You'll know the minute I do, and then..." He gave Mikal a fatherly pat on the arm before he rose to his feet. "Choices. I'll get out of your way so you can enjoy what's left of this evening." To Morgan he added, "Good night, dear lady."

With Yuri gone, Mikal reached for Morgan's hand and laced his fingers through hers. Her eyes followed the path of his arm, but she knew by the way he held her hand what look she would find when she reached his face. Still, it surprised her a little. His face was taut with an emotion that transcended desire. His eyes touched her with concern, almost compassion. She meant to ask him whether something was wrong, and her lips parted for the question, but his covered them with a hard, quick kiss. He laid his forehead against hers and whispered, "No more heavy discussions. What's left of the night belongs to us."

## Chapter Seven

He knew she'd measured his promise against the time that lay before them, and she was stalling. He listened while she told him things about herself that he already knew, or at least suspected. It was the omissions that interested him, the fact that she mentioned no close friends, no ties other than professional ones. She didn't think she needed anyone, but he believed she'd come this far because she needed him. She simply hadn't admitted that to herself yet. But she would, Mikal promised himself. Since he'd met Morgan, he'd come a long way, too.

She said she wanted to see the sights tomorrow, and he promised to take her, which meant, she said, that she needed some sleep. They walked back to their rooms with slow, heavy feet, and Morgan's brain, which had been crowded with chatter, went suddenly blank. Sleep was far from her mind, and sense seemed to be, too. She didn't turn to him at the door to say good-night, as she'd imagined herself doing. But when the door closed behind her, she turned to find that he wasn't there. Her face grew instantly hot. Staring at the Do Not Disturb sign that hung on the doorknob, she felt hollow inside.

She should have been relieved, she told herself, but as she prepared for bed she thought of going to him. She thought of what she might say and how he might respond. She wanted to be with him tonight—just be with him. She'd seen him with his son, with his uncle, with others who admired him. There were so many demands made on him, so many people who laid claim to him. His dreams were too big for her, but she wanted a piece of him anyway, some small piece of him that would be hers and no one else's. Mikal never laughed at anyone or took anyone's feelings lightly, and it would be easy to go to him and admit to this preposterous need for just one small . . .

The knock at the door between their rooms reverberated all the way to her chest. Morgan pulled the door open and found him leaning against the doorframe dressed only in a pair of jeans. "I can't sleep, lady," he said, his eyes alight at the sight of her. "You're making too much racket."

"I haven't made a sound," she told him quietly, her eyes warming to the glow in his. "It must be all in your head."

She wore a black nightgown with lace that followed the curve of her breasts, and she hadn't taken her hair down yet. He was glad. He wanted to do that for her. "You're all that's in my head." He reached out to touch her cheek with the backs of his fingers. "I want to come in."

"You're welcome," she whispered, closing her eyes and relishing his touch.

"That's not easily said, is it?"

She opened her eyes to look at him as she took his hand. "It came more easily than I thought it would."

"You've given it a great deal of thought, have you?"

"My head seems to be filled with you, too."

"But you think it shouldn't be, and I thought I shouldn't press." He stepped from his room to hers, shutting the door behind him. Light from the bathroom spilled over toward the big bed in the middle of the room.

"'Should' is such a worthless word when it comes to—"

"You should let your hair down for me." One by one, he pulled the pins from her hair until it fell down her back. He combed it with his fingers. "Beautiful. Now you should just relax."

Closing her eyes once more, she lifted her chin and breathed deeply of the scent of him, enjoying his ministrations.

He pulled her close and lowered his mouth to hers, muttering "And you should put your arms around me" before he kissed her. She complied, and then there were no more "shoulds," only "woulds." She would have this much of him now. She would make a place deep inside her practical, well-organized self, and there she would cherish her piece of this beautiful dreamer. Just one night would be all she would need, one improbable and glorious night, and then he could dream on, and she would be satisfied.

His kisses were deep, hot and wholly absorbing, drawing her in, drawing her down. The sheets cooled her back, and the broad expanse of his chest warmed her breasts. She touched him to know him, the smooth feel of his back, the tension in each muscle that shifted as he moved over her. He made her neck tingle with the touch of moist lips, and then he kissed the curve of her shoulder as he slipped the strap of her nightgown out of the way of his searching mouth. Baring one breast, he nuzzled it, tongued her nipple to make it hard, then made it his.

"Oh," she groaned appreciatively, then whispered, "Mikal."

"Don't hold back with me, Morgan." His fingers touched her covered breast in soft circles. "Show me when it's good, and let me make it better."

"It's been so long."

"Then we'll make it last." He pushed the other strap away. "We'll make it worth the wait."

"I haven't been waiting. I haven't been *wanting....*" His tongue made a diamond of the second nipple, and she caught her breath.

"You do now."

Her breast felt cool and wet after his mouth came away, but he warmed it with his breath. "I want this night with you," she confessed.

"I want your skin next to mine," he said, and took her gown away. She watched him as he looked down at her, and she knew her beauty by the light in his eyes. "I've been wanting you since we first met," he whispered, "but I had no idea..."

She was smooth, like silk, but every plane and curve of her body was firm. He'd felt that solidity whenever he'd held her in his arms, but her silkiness had been hidden beneath tailored suits, crisply creased slacks, neatly ironed blouses. He loved natural beauty, and he lowered his head to pay tribute to hers.

His hands were bold and gentle, and his mouth found exquisite ways to make her flesh tingle. The wanting in her became a fluid thing that coursed and eddied, pitched and plummeted wildly inside her, demanding some vital piece of Mikal. She slid her palms down his back until they met the waistband of his jeans.

"You're still dressed."

He chuckled. "A man needs to keep his pockets handy." Dropping a kiss at her temple, he whispered, "I came prepared to protect you."

"Thank you, Mikal." It seemed unnecessary to tell him that she hadn't been totally unprepared. "But this—" she hooked a finger in the back of his waistband "—*this* isn't fair," she groaned.

"Who said it had to be?" Raining small kisses over her face, he smoothed her hair with one hand and the satiny skin just below her navel with the other. He felt her fingers slip inside his waistband and follow its path from his back to his belly, and he sucked in a breath. "If you're looking for fairness, you won't find it that way."

"Why not?"

"Because patience doesn't seem to be my body's greatest virtue right now."

"Who said it had to be?" She managed to flick open the snap of his jeans before he hauled her hips against his, trapping her hand before it made another move, silencing her frustrated groan with his mouth, pinning her thighs in the vise of his.

"I did," he rasped, and he thought his own demands on himself might very well drive him mad. He drank her mouth's sweetness while he traced the indentation of her waist and the proud curve of her hip. His thumb strayed over her abdomen, and when she relaxed, giving in to his hypnotic caress, he released her thighs and tucked his hand between them.

Morgan gave herself over to pleasure, dimly aware that she hadn't gotten what she wanted of him yet, but that he was at least making promises. She had only to hold on to that last corner of herself, to save it for him. He eased back, and she smiled at his look of burning passion.

"You won't let go," he said.

"Not yet. Not without you. Not this time." Each refusal was tellingly breathless. She found his zipper with one hand and opened his jeans. And then she found him inside them.

When he was as naked as she, they both became desperate. He moved over her, and she lifted herself to him, welcoming the sting of his first thrust with a small whimper, absorbing the power of the second with a sigh of pleasure.

"Oh, Morgan," came as his apology.

"It's fine, Mikal. It's been..."

"...a long time. You feel so..."

"...good. And you...oh, Mikal, you're music. You're poetry, Mikal."

"We're poetry," he whispered. "Trochaic rhythm, I think. Oh, Morgan..."

"Yes, yes, *yes,* Mikal...Mikal...*Mikal!*"

The litany she made of his name matched the rhythm of the poetry he made with her. It was that piece of him she took, and while she hoarded it jealously, a similar piece of her became forever his.

It was early morning and they hadn't slept. It felt too good to lie in each other's arms and touch or catch a languid look, a satisfied smile, a soft, nuzzling kiss. And tease. The teasing was delicious, Morgan thought. He did it so sweetly. Her teasing had always had a slight edge to it, and she liked his way better. It was warmer.

"Where's that muscle you told me about?" he wondered as he slid his hand around to the back of her thigh. "The one you found when you were shaving. Flex it for me so I won't have to go prowling around looking for peepholes."

"I thought you said you'd only peek to see the expression on my face."

"I lied, of course." She raised one eyebrow in mock surprise. "A diplomatic lie. Courteous, not substantive. Come on, show me."

She stretched, tightening every muscle in her legs. "A diplomatic lie? Figures."

"Ooo, nice. That muscle was definitely worth cultivating."

"Very diplomatic."

"No, that was honest admiration, Miss Kramer." He gave her kneecap a quick kiss as he ran his hand under her calf, admiring more. Then he scooted back up. "A diplomatic lie is like when I ask how you are, and you say 'fine' whether you are or not. Or—" his blue eyes softened as he looked into hers "—when I take you too suddenly, and it hurts, but you say it's fine."

"I *was* fine. I was more than fine." She smiled to convince him.

"You have a real stubborn streak."

"Oh, yes, I do have that." She touched his hair, then laid her hand along his cheek. "It's a sanity-saver when you're dealing with dreamers."

"Ahh." He nodded, registering the idea. "Dreamers." Uncomfortable with labels and categories of any kind, Mikal chafed at this one, but he suspected she had some connection to make that might be interesting. "You've dealt with guys like me before, huh?"

"I have a positive predisposition to get tangled up with guys like you, and I don't know why." Her sigh was only for effect; the way she ran an exploratory finger around the curve of his ear and along his neck said that she wasn't minding this particular entanglement. "I don't have an impractical bone in my body."

"Hmm. You say stubbornness works well for you?" She nodded. Settling back against a pile of pillows, he folded his arms across his chest. "How so?"

"It's a good mooring. When a dreamer goes drifting away to do 'his thing,' I'm still tethered right where I want to be—on good, firm, North Dakota sod."

He smiled at the image she created of herself, the lone woman clinging to her piece of grassland, which hardly coincided with the reality of the nude beauty who was sharing the bed with him at that moment. "I wasn't trying to drift away or do *my* thing. I had your pleasure in mind."

The light was dim, but he saw that she flushed. "Yes, well...we did *our* thing, and it was certainly very...pleasurable." *And I have a piece of you, Mikal Romanov.*

"Come here," he said quietly, opening his arms for her. She slid into the pocket he made for her against his side. "How many other dreamers are we talking about here, Morgan? If it's just a couple, I wouldn't call it a positive predisposition."

"Besides my father, there was...Jeremy." The word fell into the air like a three-hundred-pound set of barbells.

"Jeremy?" He didn't like the name.

"Jeremy was an artist. I'm sure he still is—he was good at it."

"I don't suppose he had a practical bone in his body," Mikal ventured.

"Not one."

"But that isn't why you parted company."

"I admired Jeremy. I admired his work." She shrugged the shoulder that wasn't buried under Mikal's arm. "Jeremy admired Jeremy. Jeremy admired Jeremy's work." Lifting her chin, Morgan offered a confident smile. "I've learned a lot about big dreams."

"What have you learned?"

"That relationships tend to be dwarfed by them."

"I see." He saw the long, dark hair that fell over her shoulder and his arm, the soft, white breast pressed against his side, and the glittering hazel eyes that defied him to deny the truth in her statements. Mikal knew better than to argue with long-held convictions. He knew that he had to let them stand for the time being while he worked around them, gained her trust, offered himself as he was. In time she would topple those beliefs herself.

He moved his hand over her belly and smiled. "If I were an artist, I'd paint a portrait of you right now, Morgan. You'd be a masterpiece with that dewy-eyed look and those wonderful muscles." She returned the smile. "Did Jeremy ever paint your portrait?"

"No."

"Well, there it is, positive proof." Oddly relieved, Mikal turned on his side, easing down for a kiss. "The man was an absolute fool."

*  *  *

It was a balmy day, with enough crispness in the air to smack of November and enough sunshine to keep the chill at bay. Morgan loved historical sights, galleries and museums, and Mikal enjoyed seeing them with her. At the foot of the towering stairway leading to the Philadelphia art museum they eyed one another for a moment, gauged the distance and then raced one another up the steps. They arrived at the top with an exhilarated burst of laughter that caught the attention of a uniformed security guard, who wondered if they were "training for the championship."

Independence Hall was a moving experience for Morgan. Because she was an educator and a history buff, she'd always made a point of stopping at national landmarks whenever she traveled, but she found colonial Philadelphia's little state house to be more than just a place of historical interest. The rooms seemed too small to accommodate so many great men at once. She could almost feel their presence as she surveyed the assembly room with its soft colors and clean architectural lines. Washington, Jefferson, Franklin—names to be found on street signs in every corner of the country—but they had been men once, and they'd spent untold hours in these rooms. Above the voice of the park ranger who guided them through the building, Morgan could hear echoes of people arguing, haggling, coaxing and swearing, even indulging in the mundane gossip that must have filled the hours. There had been tremendous excitement here, she realized, and terrible fear.

Morgan looked up at Mikal, who stared briefly at Washington's "rising sun" chair before turning his meditative expression her way. "They say it was pretty hot that summer in more ways than one. Wonder where we'd all be if they'd decided to go back to safer moorings and hang on to what they had."

"They couldn't have done that," Morgan decided. "They came here to do a job, and they did it."

"You don't think any of them ever had the urge to call it quits—just say the hell with King George and all the rest of it, I've got a plantation to run?"

Morgan studied the carving of the sun at the top of Washington's chair. "I'm sure they had their moments, but they were made of sturdy stuff."

"Really? Strange stuffing for guys like that."

The ranger was herding his little group of tourists along, and Morgan looked up when Mikal took her arm. "What do you mean, 'guys like that'?"

A spark of mischief danced in his eyes. "Nothing but dreamers, every last one of them."

The little house where Mikal took Morgan for lunch was over two hundred years old. It was Yuri's home and one of the few free-standing houses in the old section of the city. There were plenty of row houses along the cobblestoned streets, like those on Elfreth's Alley, which seemed like a street in miniature, built, Morgan fantasized, for people who might have been only four and a half feet tall. Yuri had acquired his house a few blocks away before restoration had been the vogue. Having renovated it according to the Historical Society's standards, he now owned a valuable piece of history.

Morgan was enchanted from the minute she stepped into the tiny parlor. Two Kennedy-style rockers faced the small brick fireplace that had once been the house's main heat source. The dining area held a table, four chairs and a breakfront hutch, and the kitchen, which had once been a pantry, was only big enough for the cook, preferably someone half Mikal's size.

"I don't need gadgets," Mikal grumbled from the kitchen as Morgan set the table. "But I could use a little room to turn around."

"What are you trying to make in there?"

"Just a quick quiche," he called over his shoulder. Searching the cupboards required a great deal of leaning and ducking.

"Oh, Mikal, that's too much trouble. Besides, haven't you heard? Real men don't eat quiche."

He leaned back and stuck his head out into the dining room. "They don't? What do they eat?"

"Meat and potatoes."

"That's *it*?"

Morgan laughed. He looked as though he'd somehow wedged himself into a child's playhouse. If that shoulder didn't belong to the proverbial "real man," then there was no such thing. "Cold meat sandwiches for lunch, I think."

He ducked back into his niche with the assurance that "This kitchen isn't *that* small." As he worked, Morgan was never sure whether his conversation was meant for her or the food in preparation. "Spinach—great. And fresh mushrooms. We're in luck. Well, sort of fresh. How long have you guys been hanging out here? Hmm, not bad. You're okay." Morgan heard a couple of clattering sounds, some chopping and then a muttered curse. "What do you think about a set of decent knives as a Christmas present?"

"Me?" Or the mushrooms? Morgan wondered.

"For Uncle Yuri. These are a joke."

"Are they making the spinach cry?"

He remembered admonishing her once over her treatment of crepe batter, and he laughed. "They're making *me* cry." He craned his neck around the doorway again. "But you can make me laugh again. Come on and kiss the cook."

Morgan set the last of the silverware out and moved toward the kitchen, concerned. "Did you cut yourself?"

"Would it help if I did?"

Laying her hand on the back of his neck, she touched her lips to his in sweet consolation and then repeated, "Did you?"

"No." He smiled against her lips. "But do that again."

Her next kiss was a teasing nibble, followed by a peck. "In answer to the original question, I think knives are a very practical gift."

"Bingo!" He returned her peck with more gusto. "The magic word is practical. Fork over one more stamp of approval, and you shall feast on the very finest—'' she kissed him quickly, and he grinned ''—lips available in the City of Brotherly Love.''

''What about *sisterly* love?''

In a passable south Philly drawl he retorted, ''Hey, what about it, sister? It takes two pairs of lips—y'know what I mean? I got no problem with equal billing.''

''But you do have the very finest lips,'' she assured him, touching the lower one with her fingertip before she moved away. ''I could learn to love this wonderful old house, but it seems a little small for Yuri.''

''A refrigerator and a hot plate would be enough kitchen for Uncle Yuri. Bed, bookshelves, a roof over his head—that's about all he needs. He's gone a lot. We've got a little white wine here. How about a glass?''

''Only if it complements the quiche.'' She spotted goblets in the hutch and took two out as she wondered how soon it would be before Mikal needed as little in the way of a home as Yuri did. David would soon be old enough for a good deal of independence, and Mikal's singular talents were apparently much in demand.

''It will shower the quiche with compliments and put a little glow in your cheeks, as well.'' She held the glasses out to him, and he poured.

''Here's to brotherly love,'' she offered, glass raised.

His gaze caught hers. ''Here's to...womanly love.''

Glasses chinked. ''And real men.''

He put his arm behind her neck and drew her closer. ''Who'll take womanly love—'' he gave one soft kiss

"—over quiche—" followed by another "—anytime." He lingered longer on the third kiss.

"I'm hungry...for quiche." There was some truth in that, she told herself as her eyes drifted open. Mikal smiled and sipped his wine, and she knew he didn't doubt she was hungry.

He showed her the rest of the house—the bedroom, bathroom and den on the second floor, and the second bedroom in the garret. All the rooms were compact and efficiently furnished, and the first and second floors were connected by a narrow, winding flight of stairs. The garret was accessible only by ladder.

They were enjoying quiche, salad and a second glass of wine when Yuri let himself in the front door. Mikal knew the reason for the intrusion when he saw his uncle's expressionless face. Yuri had suggested this stop at his house for lunch, and he'd also promised Mikal some information.

"Have you children taken in all the important sights?" Yuri asked, not bothering to take off his topcoat.

"This house is one of the important sights, Yuri. It feels like living history, sort of a..." Morgan saw that Yuri had other things on his mind, and she had an uncomfortable feeling about what they might be, an unreasonable dread of hearing them. "Have you had lunch?" she asked quickly. "The quiche is delicious."

"Thank you, no. I'll interrupt for just a few moments, and then I must get back to the hotel." He beckoned Mikal with a gesture. "Just a brief conference. We've had word, Mikal."

The two men went upstairs, leaving Morgan at the table. The food was no longer palatable. She sipped her wine and tasted fear. She heard the brusque tones men used when business became serious, but the voices upstairs were too low for her to distinguish words. Secrets were to be expected in their business, Morgan told herself. They were men who looked for the skeletons in the world's closets, and there was a lot of risk-taking in such activity. She didn't want to know, didn't *need* to know, what they were talking about—except that she had a feeling. She shivered with it. Icy nausea. Their conversation touched her somehow.

On his way out Yuri pressed Morgan's hand between both of his and offered a strangely sad smile. "You and Mikal will talk. Old men always bring complications. It's the way of the world, I'm afraid."

Morgan couldn't find an airy reply, but she clung to Yuri's hand a moment longer.

Yuri turned to Mikal. "We'll count on you, then."

"Yes."

"I'll make the arrangements. You should have a couple of hours, at least."

Morgan stared at the door Yuri had closed behind him. At the touch of Mikal's hand on her shoulder, she turned and stepped into his arms and pressed the side of her face against his sweater. "May I know where you're going?"

"Yes, but you mustn't discuss it with anyone, Morgan. I'm going to an island in the Caribbean." She lifted her head to look up at him. "De Colores."

"My father is there." She took great care with the words, because she wanted them to be the simple truth. No complications from old men or younger ones.

"I know."

"But something's happened," she concluded.

Her eyes glittered up at him, and he hated the words, hated saying them to her. "There was a quick, quiet, almost bloodless coup. It looks like they've traded their old dictator in for a new one, but we're not—"

"*Almost* bloodless?"

"He's alive, Morgan. A number of Americans are being detained by the new government. Your father is one of them."

## Chapter Eight

How do you know?"

"We have reliable contacts." The fear in her eyes cut him deeply. "The details are sketchy. Nothing has been officially released on this. The State Department wants verification, and then they'll quietly notify—"

"The next of kin," she whispered.

"They're not even sure who they're dealing with, Morgan. The former regime was pro-Western, and this one, until they establish themselves . . . well, they're probably on the fence right now. We just don't know."

"What kind of people are they? Pro-Western, anti-Western—Mikal! My father is a *minister*. He has nothing to do with—"

"I know." He also knew her need to lash out.

"Why does the State Department need verification? How can your people be so sure if the State Department doesn't even know for certain?"

"We're regarded with a certain trust by some who can't trust anyone else. As I said, we have reliable—"

"Contacts, yes." The idea was incredible, and she tossed her head to make it go away. "Contacts! That's spy talk, agency talk." He lifted his hand to touch her face, but she whirled away from him. "Mikal! My father is a missionary. He has nothing to do with politics." Wild-eyed, she clenched her fists at her sides, struggling against the whole insane concept. "He has a little church and a school, and he feeds children and hands out secondhand clothing, and he doesn't... These people have guns, don't they, Mikal?"

"Morgan..."

He reached for her, but she backed away. "In the news, they always look like a bunch of thugs, and they're armed to the teeth. Are these...these *revolutionaries* like that?"

"Probably. But they're not going to hurt him, Morgan. He's no good to them dead."

"'Hurt' and 'kill' are two different things." Her voice quivered, low and gravelly, in her throat. "He's not a young man. Even so, he'll look after everyone else before he looks after himself. Mikal, if it's a choice between...he'll care more what happens to the others than..."

Her hands went to her face, and he seized the opportunity to take her back into his arms. Weeping softly, she sagged against him. "I should have gone to see him . . . just once."

"There'll be time, Morgan."

She grabbed two handfuls of his sweater and leaned back to plead, "Take me with you, Mikal."

"No."

"Let me go with you. I promise I won't—"

"No." He took her face in his hands and held her still. "Morgan, no. Truthfully, I don't know what's going on down there."

"Then what can you do? What can *you* do, Mikal Romanov? Do you have a gun?"

"No."

"*Will* you have a gun?"

"No."

"Then how will you get my father out? He doesn't have a gun, either, and *they* have . . ." She squeezed her eyes shut and saw her father with his hands bound behind his back and the barrel of a gun inches from his head. Tears rolled down her cheeks and splashed into Mikal's palms. "Oh, Mikal, please let me . . ."

"No," he whispered. "Please let *me*. Morgan, this is part of what I do."

"What can you do?" she demanded.

"I can talk to them." He saw the disbelief in her eyes. She wanted to hear that he could leap tall buildings in a single bound, crush bricks with his bare hands, shoot from the hip with precision and grace. He wished, just for her, that he could make *talk* sound as powerful. "I speak Spanish, which is one of the reasons I've been chosen."

"And you'll just . . . talk?"

He gave her half a smile. "Would you rather I promised to blow their heads off?"

"Yes."

With a quick laugh, he wrapped his arms around her. "Then I will."

"Is that one of those diplomatic lies?"

"Yes."

She closed her eyes and sighed. "Do you really have a chance, Mikal?"

"Yes. Otherwise I wouldn't go."

"You men always expect the women to stay home and wait, worrying. I don't want to be left . . ."

"I know." He tilted her head back so that she could see for herself. He understood. "Waiting is the hard part. Keep a candle burning for me, and I'll do my best to keep in touch with you." He brushed his lips across her forehead.

"Your best?" she managed, swallowing hard. Would there be problems even keeping in touch?

"Trust me, Morgan," he whispered. "Let me take care of this."

"I'm scared, Mikal." She closed her eyes and let him taste tears on her cheeks.

"Yes, I know." He drew her closer, and she tightened her hold around his back.

"I'm scared for *you*."

"I'll be all right," he promised before he closed his mouth over hers.

She strained to get closer, to be enveloped in the comfort of his confidence. His hands moved along the ridges of her back and settled over her buttocks, and he pressed her against him. They shared a long, deep shudder.

"Hold me, Mikal."

"I need you now."

"Yes. Let me take care of you."

Zippers were difficult, buttons barely manageable. Flesh was alive, warm to the touch, yielding. So little time, so much to give.

"Make me part of you, Morgan."

"That's what I want. That's what I've wanted."

"It's settled, then. That's what you'll have."

Chairs were pushed aside. A small braided rug received them. Hovering close to his face, she breathed his breath. Cradling his head to her breast, she let tears fall in his hair. And then they cradled each other.

"You can't leave me now, not really."

"Keep me here. Keep me inside you."

"You're safe here, Mikal. Always."


The door between their rooms had been left open. There wasn't much time, and while she packed, Morgan listened to the sounds coming from Mikal's room, doting on them. Minutes were precious. She tossed things in her bags and turned from the shoddy job she'd done to find that Mikal had done much the same. Going to his aid, she assumed charge of the tuxedo he was stuffing into a garment bag. "I'll take this with me," she decided. "It'll just be in your way."

"Thanks." He backed away as she took over, smoothing, straightening, fussing over his shirts and pants as though taking care of an untidy child. Mikal shoved his hands into his pockets, lifting one corner of his mouth in a smile. She needed to be busy. "That leaves a little room for that stuff over there."

Morgan reached for the big plastic shopping bag that lay next to Mikal's small suitcase. "New clothes?"

"Summer stuff. Uncle Yuri thinks of everything."

"I'm glad someone does." She emptied the bag on the bed and began removing tags from the short-sleeved shirts and lightweight pants. She held up a sporty cotton jacket. "Is this the proper negotiator's attire? This looks like something for the well-dressed African explorer."

"I don't know much about styles." He chuckled as he lifted the jacket's sleeve. "David would get a kick out of this. He's been critical of my jackets with the elbow patches, says I oughta get with it. What do you think? Is this 'with it'?"

She imagined him wearing the natural-colored cottons and smiled. "If it isn't, I'm sure you can set a new trend."

"You'll look in on him, won't you?" She glanced at Mikal, saw the worry in his eyes, and she nodded. "Not just at school. His Aunt Peg's not too crazy about any of this, and she'll be huffing and puffing around. He'll need to be able to talk to someone else."

"You've called him?"

"Yes. I told him as much as I knew—more than I've told him before. He's too old to be satisfied with the promise of a souvenir."

"What did he say?"

Mikal smiled, pride brightening his eyes. "He told me to give 'em hell. I think he'd like me to pack a gun, too."

It was Morgan who took Mikal's hands and held them in hers. He would bring her father home. No weapon could match what Mikal had. He was going not because he sought the challenge, but because it sought him. The man that he was couldn't *not* go.

When the phone rang they both flinched. She held his hands a moment longer but on the fourth ring he answered. There was no conversation, just Mikal's confirmation. He was nearly ready. Morgan finished his packing quickly, touching each piece of his clothing in the silent hope that when he wore it, something of her would be close to his skin. Each item that was his seemed precious. She had a wild notion that she should pack a lunch for him, knit him some socks, or give him her ring. They were the most feminine of drives—to feed a man, keep him warm, give him remembrances. She was surprised to find she had those drives in her and, for some reason, she was pleased.

"I'll be in touch," he promised. "Often. And when I come back, I'll want to see you." He pulled her into his arms and kissed her. She held tight as he whispered, "Immediately. And then often. Do you think that can be arranged?"

"I think you could arrange to have the sun rise in the west, Mikal. With that silver tongue of yours..."

With a growl, he pressed his lips to the side of her neck and then gently corrected, "Velvet tongue, sweet

Morgan. While I'm gone, decide which parts of your beautiful being would most enjoy the touch of velvet.''

While he was gone, she decided that every part of her being wanted him back home. Without fanfare or media coverage, Mikal and Yuri had left Philadelphia on a plane bound for Mexico City en route to De Colores. As she said goodbye, Morgan told herself that Mikal would bring her father back. A piece of cake for the Romanovs, she decided, a routine matter. Pull a few strings, smooth a few feathers, the right words in the right ears, and everything would be all right. It was her part that would be the most difficult to play—waiting.

In two weeks there had been two calls from Mikal. The first came from Mexico City. Mikal and Yuri were leaving for La Primavera, De Colores's capital city, by chartered plane.

"Listen, Morgan, if I can't put my calls through directly, I'll get word to you by the Red Cross. And to David through you. Okay?''

Her stomach twisted into a knot. She knew he was saying that if his mission went awry, he wanted David to get the news from her rather than from some stranger. When word had come from the State Department that her father had been "detained," Morgan was glad she already knew, glad that the initial word had come from Mikal.

"David stopped in to see me this afternoon." She tossed off a small laugh. "He seems to think you timed this Caribbean junket just right. The weather's just turned cold.'' Morgan tried to will the tension in her stomach away. They *volunteered* for this, she told herself. Both her father and Mikal. This was who they were, and loving them meant sitting around with her insides tied up in knots, which was not the way she intended to live the rest of her life. She would definitely cut back on loving them, both of them, when they were safe.

Though the temperature was eighty-seven degrees in Mexico, Mikal felt the cold, and he felt the knot in her stomach. ''Are you cold, Morgan?''

''Yes,'' she said quietly. ''Yes,'' she repeated, injecting more strength into the word. ''But I'm going to turn up the heat and have a cup of tea. And I'm not going to worry, Mikal. I know you'll be successful.''

''I like your outlook. I'll try not to enjoy the weather too much if you'll just remember...'' Remember the sound of my voice and how you felt when you looked at me when we were alone together, how you felt when I held you, and remember '' . . . to keep a candle burning for me.''

''I'll do that, Mikal. I promise.''

Two days later Morgan received a call from the Red Cross. ''Mr. Romanov sends word that he has reached his destination and his business should be taken care of within a few days.''

Those few days were already long past by Morgan's calculations. She had acquired the habit of eating dinner alone by candlelight, a touch that she told herself was a pleasant one, but essentially meaningless.

Pleasant, too, were the candles on the mantel and in the hurricane lamps by the mirror in the entryway. She'd never lit them since she'd first hung them on the wall, but now she decided she liked to keep the light flickering inside the glass. After all, Christmas was coming, and that was the time for candles.

News of the De Colores situation was vague. Everyone seemed to be sizing up the new government, which made bold declarations of its independence. Most foreigners had been free to leave the island or stay, as they wished. Transportation problems had caused some delays in evacuation, and there were those, a few American citizens among them, who were being temporarily detained by the new government, but no mention of hostages was ever made in the media. Nor was there mention of Freedom International.

"How come he can't call us himself, then?" David demanded as he scowled at Morgan's TV screen while they watched the evening news.

"Maybe tonight he will." Morgan gave David a hopeful smile. He'd been coming over in the evenings for the past week, hoping to be there when the next call came.

"You know what he'll do, don't you? He'll just park himself on the steps of the presidential palace and wait till hell freezes over or they let those people go." With a sigh, David tossed a magazine back on the coffee table where he'd found it. "That's just the way he is. He'll get himself—" David glanced at Morgan and slouched down a little further. He felt pretty low. "I'm sorry. I know it's for your dad."

"And I know it's your dad you're worrying about, so I guess we're both in the same boat."

"All these candles remind me of one of his damn rallies." David cast another guilty glance at Morgan and slid down further. "I mean *crazy* rallies. I mean... I don't know what I mean. He does such *good* stuff, but geez..."

"You want him back here, safe and sound." Morgan's encouraging nod gave David leave to agree. "I do, too."

She meant she wanted them *both* back, and David knew that. She'd been concerned for her father and his these last weeks, and he wondered if she were as scared as he was. He searched her sympathetic expression for signs. "It's usually the guys who are dying to punch somebody's face in who won't back down," he began. "Dad's the most peaceful guy you'll ever meet, but he won't give an inch, not on something like this. What I don't understand is, if you're not willing to punch out somebody's lights, how do you make him give in?"

"I guess you try to persuade him to look at things from your perspective," Morgan suggested as she folded her arms. "Which the adversary probably couldn't manage if his lights were punched out."

"Yeah, but sometimes..." His attention seemed to be drawn back to the news for a moment. He took a long drink from the cup of hot chocolate he'd been nursing as he watched. "You know, I saw a TV special about the sixties, and they showed some film clips of the '68 Democratic convention. My dad was there—he was just a college kid—and sure enough, I saw him in that show. I was just sitting there watching this riot stuff, and all of a sudden there's my dad, being beaten with a club. I swear, Dad was twice as big as that cop, but he didn't fight back. He was trying to shield some other guy with his own body, when he could have just taken that club away and broken it over the cop's head.'' He mimed the motions, then turned to Morgan with a face full of conviction. ''He could have, you know.''

''I'm sure he could have, but then he'd have gotten himself arrested.'' She used her sensible teacher's tone for David's sake. She knew her role. But the mental image of Mikal being beaten made her mad as hell.

''He got arrested anyway. The camera picked that up, too. I wanted to walk into that film and fight back for him.''

Morgan laughed. ''You weren't even born yet!''

''Yeah, I know. Wouldn't it have been great? An avenging angel from the future comes back to make mincemeat out of—'' Grinning, David shook his head. ''But you know what? He'd probably have protected the cop from *me*. He's gotten arrested a couple of times for protesting, but when he believes in something... You know, when they organize those demonstrations, the people who get arrested are usually volunteers.''

''Yes, I know.'' She'd been in on one, she remembered, a long time ago. Teachers demonstrating at the

White House. She remembered being told that there would be arrests, and she had been relieved to learn that it was part of the strategy; *she* would not be arrested. She felt a pang of inexplicable guilt.

"I guess...I guess that's just Dad," David decided. "He wouldn't be Dad if he didn't care so hard."

"Care so *hard*?"

"Well, it's hard—it's *hard* getting hit over the head with a club."

"And not fighting back?" Morgan asked gently.

"Yeah, especially when you know just one good right would..." David smacked his fist into his palm, and they both laughed at the irony. David might do that. Morgan, maybe. But not Mikal. "He's not gonna change, is he? He's gonna keep on being just as weird as he's always been." Morgan nodded. "I'm glad," David concluded. "I love him just like he is."

He looked at Morgan to see if she felt the same way. The funny way her eyes glistened as she smiled made him think she probably did.

Morgan wasn't sure when she decided to go to De Colores on her own. It might have been on the spur of the moment when the Red Cross told her that they were "not currently in touch" with either Mikal or Yuri Romanov, even though conditions on the island appeared stable. It might have been on the heels of the frustrating telephone conversation with a Mr. Morris at the State Department, who assured her that he would hear if her father's situation became critical, and since he hadn't heard, it must not be. The word "hostage" met with resounding disapproval from Mr. Morris. She might have decided when she'd reread her father's last letter, or Mikal's poetry. Ultimately it might have been David's courage that activated a little of her own. It was an impetuous move, the kind she almost never made, but when the pilot announced the little commuter plane's arrival at La Primavera, Morgan's blood surged with excitement.

The air was warm and heavy, and its salty scent captured Morgan's fancy. The sea was visible from the small landing strip, and the stretch of white sand made her wish she were on vacation. White runway, white buildings, white-capped sea and white sand—the reflected light from the noon sun was almost oppressive. Morgan followed the other passengers to the terminal.

To her surprise, the customs official let her pass with few questions. She explained that she was on vacation in Mexico, and she claimed to have friends in De Colores who worked for the Red Cross. In fact she had two names, and those seemed acceptable. The new government obviously hoped that tourism would flourish again in short order because the official said that the beaches were beautiful this time of year. Then he asked about the weather in North Dakota as he stamped her passport.

With her two small bags in hand, Morgan breathed a sigh of relief as she made her way to the street outside the small terminal. One hurdle cleared. She refused to worry about the military jeep, the canvas-covered truck and the four leering men, armed and dressed in fatigues, whose suggestions to her were clearly understandable even though she spoke no Spanish.

She took a taxi to the Red Cross office, which was adjacent to the island's one hospital. It wasn't much of a hospital, Morgan decided as she surveyed the two-story stucco building. She had higher hopes for the Red Cross, which was housed in a newer, cleaner-looking building. It was the only contact she had.

"I'm trying to locate two American citizens who are here on the island somewhere. I wonder if you can help me."

The woman behind the desk reminded Morgan of a prairie grouse, so perfectly did she blend with her surroundings—gray dress and gray hair, which matched the steel-gray desk and file cabinet and the gray walls. She looked up and offered a tight smile. "You're here under whose auspices?"

"My own," Morgan explained. "That is, I came on my own. My name is Morgan Kramer, and I'm looking for—"

The gray woman frowned. "Morgan Kramer? Have we relayed messages to you recently, Miss Kramer?"

"Yes, you have. From—"

The woman rose quickly. "Yes, I know. It was your own idea to come here?"

"Yes, I...I decided it wouldn't hurt to try. I wasn't getting any answers, and I—"

"Come with me, Miss Kramer." The woman indicated a path through the office, past crates and boxes of supplies marked with the familiar red cross, to a door in the back of the room. "I have a feeling you're going to be sent home," the gray woman mumbled as she rapped on the door.

A man's voice answered. "Yes, Dorothy?"

"We have a visitor."

The door opened, and Morgan half expected to see Mikal. Her heart sank at the sight of the granite-faced man whose crinkled eyebrows almost made her swallow her resolve. "Visitor?" The frown eased from his face as the man surveyed Morgan with all the subtlety of a panther, to which she decided he could well have been akin. "I think you got off at the wrong stop, ma'am. Bermuda is east of here."

"I'm looking for someone," Morgan informed him crisply.

The man sighed and shoved his hands in the pockets of his khaki slacks. "Well, the list is pretty long at the moment, but I guess I can—"

"Mikal Romanov," Morgan said. "And Sidney Kramer. Are they being held—"

The frown returned abruptly. "Who the hell are you?"

"My name is Morgan Kramer. Reverend Kramer is my father, and Mikal is here because—"

The man with the dark scowl snatched Morgan by the arm and dragged her through the door, muttering, "Mike's girlfriend. God in heaven, what next?"

## Chapter Nine

Take a seat, Morgan. Anywhere is fine. Mind if I smoke?''

There was only one chair in the little cubicle that appeared to be the man's office. It stood behind a desk, near a small window and the back door. With that escape route handy, it seemed a good place to situate herself. "Yes, I do." The man looked surprised, but his hand dropped away from his breast pocket. "Since you seem to know something about Mikal and me, may I know who you are?"

He smiled, and his face was no longer frightening. "'May I know who you are?' You remind me of a girl I knew in Springfield. Teacher type."

"Really," she managed tightly. "There are lots of Springfields."

"And lots of girls in every one. The name's Mc-Quade," he said, offering his hand. Morgan hesitated. "Mike's a friend of mine. His messages to you came through me."

Morgan accepted his handshake with sudden gratitude. Here was a link to Mikal. "You've seen him, then? He's all right?"

"It's been more than a week since they've allowed us any contact with them. Mike and Yuri are 'guests' at the palace—at least, they were as of a week and a half ago. Your father and the others have been detained."

"Which means?"

McQuade sat on the edge of the desk and looked Morgan straight in the eye. "Which could mean anything. This is a brand-new government, which is just like a brand-new baby. We await their pleasure. And right now, they seem to be taking pleasure in keeping us waiting."

"So you just sit here?" she asked, indicating the confines of the little office.

McQuade was amused. "I suppose you came all the way from North Dakota with a better idea?"

"Well, I...I suppose I'd..." Morgan sputtered before she remembered David's suggestion, which seemed as good as any at the moment. "I guess I'll sit on the steps of that palace until they let those people go or hell freezes over, whichever comes first."

"You're sure to draw a crowd, if nothing else."

Her jaw was set, her eyes growing colder by the minute. "Have you seen my father?"

"No."

"Do you know whether he's all right? When they plan to let him go?" McQuade shook his head. "Well, can you find out?"

"Mike Romanov is over there trying to do just that."

"And you don't even know whether Mikal is all right. Where are all of these reliable contacts of yours, Mr. McQuade?"

"Contacts of *mine*?"

"Mikal says you people have such good contacts, but you can't even seem to stay in contact with your own—"

McQuade raised a hand to quell her accusations in midstream. "First of all, I'm not part of Freedom International, even though I work with them occasionally. If Mike mentioned reliable contacts, you're probably looking at them."

It was Morgan's turn to scowl. "Oh, great. So being a contact means you're just waiting to be contacted. What an absurd situation." She rose from her chair.

"Where do you think you're going?" he asked, still amused.

"You said that Mikal is a 'guest'—" the word was couched in sarcasm "—at the palace, the seat of this glorious new government, I presume. That's where I'll try next."

"Try what? Getting yourself arrested?"

"Try getting in to see someone who will tell me something about—"

"Look, lady, simmer down." His gesture indicated that she should *sit* down, as well, and she complied. "Mikal tells me that Bismarck is one of the few places left in the world where people can leave their doors unlocked and odds are they won't get ripped off, so your naïveté is forgiven."

"Naïveté!"

"But if you screw up his efforts and get anybody killed, especially him, you won't be forgiven, so let's be friends. I don't know whatever possessed you to come to De Colores, but as long as you're here, I'll try to help you. You and I will get into that palace together." Morgan settled back into the chair and nodded. "They've been putting me off for over a week now, but they'll let me back in sooner or later, because sooner or later they'll want a good report from the Red Cross."

"You work for the Red Cross, then."

"Not exactly. Let's say I'm working *with* the Red Cross right now, and let's say you're with Freedom International. You're, uh, you're Mike's secretary."

"I don't speak Spanish."

McQuade shrugged. "Yeah, well Mike...Mike doesn't type well. What the hell, it's worth a shot."

For two days they had met with human stone walls at the doors of the presidential palace. No one knew anything about anyone named Romanov or Kramer, no one spoke Morgan's English or McQuade's Spanish, and no one was authorized to disturb anyone who might be able to answer any of their questions. Morgan was ready to stage her promised sit-in on the steps, and McQuade was on the verge of charging the entrance with a Sherman tank, when suddenly doors began to open. Glancing at one another as they followed their escort into the palace, they wondered what magic words they had said.

"We've missed your smiling face, McQuade." The announcement came from a man whose striking Latin features were enhanced by his crisp khaki uniform. His dark eyes brightened as they passed over McQuade's stony countenance and rested on Morgan. "But I see why you've been too busy to pay us a visit in the last week. The Red Cross has yet to send us such—"

"Too busy!" McQuade exploded. "I've been getting the runaround from your goons at the gate for nearly two weeks, Colonel. What the hell is going on here? Why have I been refused admittance?"

The colonel looked genuinely puzzled. "I wasn't informed of your visits."

"And I was told that you were not to be disturbed," McQuade bit out. "Which *I* found very disturbing. Are your 'guests' receiving hospitable treatment?"

"Of course."

"May I be allowed to verify that?"

"Certainly. Mikal is with the general at the moment, and Yuri chooses to spend most of his time with our detainees. That, of course, is his privilege.

Please—'' he gestured toward an open door ''—make yourselves comfortable. They have spent the morning together, and the general will need a rest soon. The young lady is . . . ?''

''Mikal's secretary,'' McQuade explained. ''Morgan Remark. Morgan, this is Colonel Hidalgo.''

''How do you do, Colonel?'' Sliding McQuade a quick frown as she offered her hand, Morgan fully expected the colonel to kiss it, but she realized she'd seen too many movies when he merely gave her a polite handshake.

''Ordinarily Miss Remark accompanies Mikal on all his missions, but we had assumed that this one would be handled quickly.'' They'd moved from a foyer to a room containing a heavy wooden table surrounded by chairs. McQuade knew the routine. He pulled a chair out for Morgan, then took the one beside her.

''Mikal's messages for his family have not reached you in the last few days, then,'' Colonel Hidalgo surmised in his accented but flawless English.

''His family hasn't had a message in almost two weeks,'' McQuade said.

The colonel's apology was directed at Morgan. ''I'm sure his loved ones are concerned about him. I regret that. We have no intention of frightening or harming anyone.''

''That *is* good news,'' Morgan told him as she assumed a collected posture, folding her hands on the table in front of her.

''Just a few moments, then,'' the colonel promised as he took his leave.

*"Remark?"* Morgan whispered, sagging a little in relief at having gotten this far.

"Kramer backward," McQuade explained with a smile. "No offense. It's best not to give them any emotions to play with, so don't let them see any. You're nobody's relative."

McQuade was pacing by the time Colonel Hidalgo finally ushered Mikal through the door. Morgan remembered packing the yellow, cotton, short-sleeved shirt and beige slacks he was wearing. He looked tired, she thought as her heart yearned toward him. He saw McQuade first. "Where've you been, McQuade? I understand you brought my sec—" the sudden sight of Morgan made him break the word into senseless pieces "—re...tary. Morgan?"

They exchanged wordless looks, one stunned, one scared, letting reality gradually take hold and giving McQuade the moment he needed. "Your home office decided you might need Miss Remark if this is to be a long siege. For, uh, correspondence, research, whatever it is you guys do. Anyway, they sent her along, and I brought her over."

"Thank you, McQuade," Mikal managed. It didn't matter for the moment that she was in danger up to her eyebrows. In her pristine white suit, hair done up to keep her neck cool, she was a vision of beauty.

"I spoke with your son just before I left," Morgan offered, finding the nerve for a tentative smile. "He's fine. He—" she cast a quick glance at Colonel Hidalgo "—hopes you'll be home for Christmas."

The fact that she was actually there in the room with him made everything else seem slightly fuzzy, out of focus. There was no floor, no furniture, nothing but Morgan. Mikal forced himself to walk calmly to the table and take the chair across from her.

"With the two of you here and no word from you," Morgan hastened to explain, "no hint of when you might be finished with your mission, we're sort of at a standstill. Loose ends, you might say."

So beautiful, he thought. Such a breath of fresh air. Invigorating, like a prairie wind. If they let you walk out of here, Morgan, don't stop walking until the plane lands in Bismarck. But if they don't...oh, God, Morgan, if they don't... You, of all people.

"We had to be certain you were all right, Mikal." She'd never seen him angry, and she wondered if the strange look on his face was his version of it. Disapproval was certainly there, and tension. But he seemed to be all right, and if something was wrong, maybe it was... "And we've had no word on the others—those who were taken...before."

"Yuri is with the detainees as our observer," Mikal explained quietly. "They're all accounted for, and Colonel Hidalgo personally sees to it that their needs are met." Morgan gave the colonel a furtive glance. He was standing at the window, pretending to have no interest in the conversation. He seemed fairly considerate, Morgan decided, for a thug who took hostages.

"There's adequate food and medical attention, then?" McQuade put in, playing his role. Mikal's chin dipped in assent. "You're not still drinking the water, are you, Mike?"

"I've come to an understanding with the water, and I'm doing my own cooking." It was difficult not to reach across the table and touch her. "It's good that you were able to see me for yourself, Morgan. Now your job will be to set the minds back home at rest. Go back to—"

"You've been ill?" she asked, more anxiously than she'd intended.

"No, no, I'm fine." Her hands were folded demurely on the table, and Mikal's own hand rose reflexively, then fell back in his lap. God, how he wanted to touch her, just her hand. But he had to send her away, and she had to go directly. He was walking on eggshells as it was. Hidalgo was one thing, but Guerrero, General Castillo's hatchet-faced enforcer, was something else. Mikal leaned forward and willed her to understand the gravity of the situation. "There's really not much you can do for me here. I need you back on the home front, holding down the fort."

Morgan dug her heels in. She'd come this far and she was not going back to the waiting routine. She searched for a plausible line. "There are several pressing matters to be discussed, Mikal. I need direction. The Levine matter has reached a critical stage, and besides that..." She looked to the colonel, who had turned from the window to take a pointed interest in the conversation. "We've been out of touch with Mikal and Yuri Romanov for almost two weeks, Colonel. Our organization simply cannot function this way. If you could allow me some time here, just to work on some details that have nothing to do with—''

Mikal's hand shot across the table and he squeezed her forearm to silence her. ''There's no need for that. Give me a written briefing, and I'll get back to you in writing or by phone—whatever I can manage.''

Colonel Hidalgo took a step nearer the table. ''You must understand, Miss Remark, that we are in the process of determining who our friends are. We allow very limited access to the palace, but if you have a reason to be here...''

''She has no reason to be here, Colonel.'' Mikal pushed himself away from the table and came to his feet, towering over everyone else in the room. ''She's just a secretary.'' He gave Morgan the first chilling look she'd ever received from him. ''Indispensable at the typewriter, but you know how it is with women. They start thinking you can't tie your shoes without their help.''

Morgan found Hidalgo's slow smile only slightly less aggravating than Mikal's comment, but at least it was warmer than the hand Mikal had laid on her arm. ''She came a long way just to tie your shoes, Mikal.'' He turned to McQuade, who had become an impartial observer, and nodded toward the door. ''I could use five minutes of your time, McQuade.''

When the door closed behind the two men, Morgan wondered whether she was, even then, truly alone with Mikal. Was there a microphone in the bookshelf? A tape recorder behind the wall? Stiff and impassive, he stood there and stared down at her. She came to her feet, hoping to minimize her disadvantage, and waited for some indication that it was safe to talk.

He spoke slowly and deliberately. "What, in the name of all that's sensible and practical, are you doing here, Morgan?"

Her hands fluttered a little. "I'm not sure. I wasn't certain how far I could get, but each time I made it a step closer, I decided I'd try one more."

"Why?"

She looked up at him, amazed. Where was the sensitivity that had been his hallmark? Why wasn't he as relieved to see her as she was to see him? "Because my father is here, and you're here, and no one knew whether either of you was safe."

"Your father is safe, and you did well not to reveal any relationships. We're walking a very thin line here, with some volatile personalities." He worked to tighten his internal hold on his emotions, reminding himself that it would be a mistake to take her in his arms.

"Hidalgo?" she asked.

"No. General Castillo has two advisers. Hidalgo is the voice of sanity here. It's Colonel Guerrero's influence that we're working to overcome."

"Are you free to walk out of here, Mikal?"

His shoulders sagged a bit. "No. Not without the others."

"Is that *your* choice?"

He shoved his hands in his pockets. "It was my choice to come here. I wasn't 'detained' like the oth-

ers. But, no, I'm not free to come and go as I please."
He gave her a hard look. "You won't be, either, if
Guerrero finds out anything about you. He thinks he
can rule the world with an M-16."

"Do you think they're watching us now?" she
whispered. "Listening?" He shook his head, and she
wanted to say "Touch me, then," but she recalled how
cold his fingertips had been and she chose reason over
emotion. "I'm going to ask the colonel to let me see
you on a daily basis, just for a few minutes, just to
assure our organization that you're safe and well. It
would be in their own best interest to—"

"You'll do no such thing. You're walking out of
here in three more minutes, Morgan, and you're not
looking back until the plane takes off with you on it."
Because he saw no sign of agreement on her face, he
took her shoulders in both hands to shake her, to
communicate his desperation. "You've got to get out
of here. I don't want you here. I don't want to see you
every day. I don't want . . ." Because he had touched
her, he was lost. He pulled her into his arms and laid
his cheek against her hair. "Oh, God, you're the most
beautiful sight I've seen since I left Philly, but you
can't be here, Morgan."

"Who says?" Her voice was raspy. Her throat
burned as she reached around to offer a crushing embrace of her own.

"Your boss says." He slipped his hand beneath her
short jacket and smoothed the cotton blouse that
covered her back. "How much am I paying this invaluable secretary who types and ties shoes?"

"Nothing." Her lips grazed his neck, and she whispered, "So I've come to get a raise out of you."

He tightened his hold on her and growled near her ear, "If not a raise, certainly a *rise* out of me." Stretching to her toes, she rubbed herself against him with all the subtlety of a hungry cat, and he groaned. "Morgan, five minutes isn't enough, and you have to go." He caressed her back, trying to get his fill of her without touching her intimately as he longed to do.

"It's so warm here. Why are your hands cold?"

Gripping her shoulders, he put her away from him, letting her see his regret. "Because I've been cold with fear since I walked into the room and found you here, Morgan. I can't believe you did something this crazy."

"I can't believe my father's a hostage, or a detainee, or whatever the latest word for it is. I can't believe we're together on this lovely little island, and we can't go down to the beach and lie in the sun." She reached up to cup his cheek in her hand. "You look as though you haven't had much sun recently. You have been ill, haven't you?"

He shrugged, letting his hands slide the length of her arms to hold her hands. "I knew better than to drink the water, but I forgot about ice cubes. Listen, I'm okay. I want you to go back and tell David that."

"Mikal, I'm not—" The door behind her opened slowly as Mikal released her hands.

"Please don't argue," he said quickly.

Colonel Hidalgo cleared his throat. "I will have someone see you and McQuade to the gate, Miss Remark."

Morgan turned, knowing that Hidalgo and Mc-Quade were waiting. She couldn't leave without looking back, but his expression was impassive once again. "I'll be back in the States very soon," he told her. "Meanwhile, let's put everything on hold." She nodded and walked out without saying goodbye.

"Would you like to have your 'secretary' with you, Mikal?" Mikal turned from the tall, narrow window. He was beginning to regard Hidalgo as his ally, and he knew that the man had not been fooled. "It could be arranged," the colonel promised.

"You could also arrange to have her flown out of here this afternoon."

Hidalgo arched an eyebrow. "You don't think she'll leave on her own?"

Mikal sighed, shaking his head in wonder at what she had accomplished already. "I don't know. I would never have expected her to take such a risk. Ordinarily she's a very sensible woman."

"A paradox, then. That makes her a fascinating woman—the only kind that would interest a man like Mikal Romanov. And, of course, she's beautiful."

"She won't be detained," Mikal insisted in a quiet, even tone. "She'll be free to go."

"If she chooses to leave, I see no problem at this point."

"But you won't arrange for her departure, either," Mikal concluded.

Hidalgo smiled, his dark eyes sparkling. "I admire her ingenuity. It will be interesting to watch her next move."

It was not McQuade's habit to try to influence a decision that wasn't his to make. He made his living working for people who were determined to beat the odds, and he seldom discouraged them from trying. Morgan Kramer had no intention of leaving the island yet, and McQuade didn't argue with her. He helped her find a room at La Casa Blanca, which was a comfortable hotel. He made inquiries for her, and he served as a sounding board. Two days after their visit to the palace, McQuade headed for the hotel with an offer from Hidalgo, and he knew Morgan wouldn't be asking for advice once she heard what he had to say.

Mike had described her as "a sensible, practical woman," and McQuade would have agreed, to a point. She had a way of making everything she did sound practical, and he had no doubt she'd convinced herself that it was perfectly sensible for a naive teacher type from the Midwest to fly down to De Colores and pretend there was something she could do about the hostages in the palace. It amused McQuade that she worked so hard at this sensible posture when it was as plain as the nose on her face that she was there because her heart wouldn't let her be anywhere else. Knowing Mikal Romanov, whom he considered to be the most admirable man he'd ever met, McQuade understood Morgan's predicament. As long as

Mike was on the island, McQuade felt that he couldn't be anywhere else, either.

Within the hour McQuade was sharing a table in the hotel lounge with Morgan. He'd already drained one beer and was starting on another. She was still sipping on a soft drink when he launched his news. "Mike seems to trust Hidalgo, so I guess we can, too. I just got word that you can go over there this evening and see Mike if you want. The invitation came from Hidalgo."

Morgan's eyes widened as she let the plastic straw slip from her lips. "If I *want*! When? What time?"

"Simmer down, now. I'll be taking you over. I want to see Hidalgo's face—make sure I'm delivering you into his hands. So we'll go in a little while."

At the thought Morgan's heart rate jumped into a higher gear. "If we have a chance to talk privately, I should be able to get a clearer picture of where Mikal's negotiations stand, and I can report back—"

"Report back?" McQuade laughed. "You're going in there to see Mike, lady. I'm not *sending* you in there, and I don't even know whether to expect you back or not."

Morgan looked incredulous. "But it's important that we establish better contact and let the State Department or somebody know where things stand."

"Yeah, well, I have a feeling the State Department has some idea. What Mike's doing is being done quietly, which is the best way to keep people alive in a situation like this." Stabbing a finger in the air for emphasis, McQuade leaned toward Morgan. "You,

Miss Remark, are going in there to see Mike. I don't know what kind of visit it will be, and I figure it's none of my business, but don't think I'm sending you, and don't think of yourself as some kind of envoy. You're not. You want to see Mike? You're getting your chance."

Morgan studied the candle that burned between them. "You don't mince words, do you, McQuade?"

"I don't see any point in it when we're all voluntarily perched up here, straddling the cutting edge of somebody else's blade. You and I know damn well that as long as we stay here, they can come and get us any time they want. We ought to be honest with ourselves about our reasons for being here." She looked up at him, and he smiled. "That makes it easier to be honest with each other about how we want to proceed. You want to change your clothes before we go?"

"Yes," Morgan said quietly, offering no smile in return.

Mikal waited in the shadows of the garden, where he could see the terrace and the door she would come through. There was a silver slip of Caribbean moon in the sky, and the garden was sweet with floral fragrance. If he couldn't give her an afternoon at the beach, he could give her a rendezvous in a tropical garden. Hidalgo had told him that she had stayed and that she continued to try to see him. If she wouldn't leave, he couldn't keep her safe. They could pick her up any time. And if Guerrero found out who she was and why she was there, he might do just that. If, if, if—she had to know, had to be warned, had to come to her senses.

And he had to see her, had to touch her, had to fill his head with the sound of her voice. For two nights he'd lain awake thinking of nothing else.

The light in the atrium came on and Mikal could see her with Hidalgo, who ushered her through the French doors to the terrace. Then the other man went back inside and closed the door and the light went out.

There she stood, her long, dark hair bright with moonlight, her white dress a beacon. Mikal indulged his senses in watching her as she crossed the tiled terrace toward the reflecting pool. The singing of insects seemed to fade for the moment as her sandals made a delicate clicking sound in the quiet of the night. Her dress was soft and loose, and it fluttered with the night breeze as she walked, as did her hair. She'd left it down, the way he liked it best.

Near the reflecting pool stood a shrine with a small mahogany carving of some saint—one whom Mikal imagined had taken pity on him this night, so he had filled the little candle holders and lit two dozen candles. Their bobbing flames, sheltered by flowering greenery, were reflected in the pool among the water hyacinths. The shrine drew Morgan, as Mikal had known it would.

She was made for candlelight. He watched her take an unlit candle from the rack and touch its wick to one of the flames he had put there to greet her. Light and shadow caressed her face, and the white spikelike flowers of an acacia fluttered around her head, pay-

ing her tribute with their sweet scent as she set the
white taper in one of the few remaining holders.

"I hope that one's for me." Morgan looked up and
saw him standing in the shadows. He always seemed
comfortable with his surroundings; his smile came
easily, as always. Morgan felt tension ease from her
stomach, and her eyes brightened with her smile. In his
white bush jacket and slacks, he could have been an
advertisement for a safari vacation. "I've been keeping him in candles for weeks now," Mikal said. "Figured I needed a friend."

"You have me," she said, her voice barely audible.
"I've kept your candle burning, just as you asked."

"I know," he whispered. "I've felt it." He reached
for her hand and pulled her into the shelter of a stand
of fringed palms. Lacing his fingers through hers, he
teased the hollows of her palms with his thumbs while
he poured fiery, slow, open kisses over her upturned
face and whispered, "Hottest . . . damned . . . flame . . .
oh, Morgan, you should go, you should go. . . ." He
tasted her temple with the tip of his tongue, and she
shivered with a thrill that passed to his own body.
"Stay, please stay, Morgan. . . . Morgan . . ."

His mouth captured hers and held it, offering no
quarter. He plundered her with his flickering, plung-
ing tongue, and she caught her breath, shocked,
singed, seduced. She felt his heat, and she arched into
it with a small sound, proclaiming her own tart, belly-
puckering need, sweet, breast-swelling need. This was
Mikal, whose way was always gentle; this was Mikal,

whose strength ran deeper than the corded muscle she caressed from waist to shoulder. What dream could match the sound of his quickened breathing, the touch of his hand, or the taste of his kiss? Morgan was grounded in reality, and she would have Mikal ground himself in her.

Morgan's cotton gauze dress moved easily beneath his hands as Mikal reveled in the feel of her. She wore something between the dress and her skin, something smooth and feminine, something that didn't bind the firm curves of her bottom or the softness of her breasts that were pressed tightly against him. With both hands he held her hips closer to himself, and she rose on tiptoe to accommodate him as she invited him to deepen their kiss. Perhaps, he thought fleetingly, he would let her drive him to distraction, and then he could enjoy this heightened awareness of her to infinity.

Mikal lifted his head at last with a tortured groan. "Morgan, you're not safe here," he rasped.

Then she knew that for her there could be no safety. She pressed moist lips high on his chest in the vee of the shirt he wore with the short-sleeved jacket.

"I'm a selfish man. I know I should talk them into arresting you and putting you on a plane bound for the States," he whispered, but his embrace didn't slacken. "What's wrong with me? Why can't I do that?"

"I've come too far," she whispered.

"So have I," he confessed, cradling her face in his hands and tilting it up to his. "Forgive me for allowing you to risk this."

"You take your risks; I'll take mine." And she kissed him again. She fastened her senses on him, ignoring the scent of gardenias and the call of a night bird. She wanted only to fill herself with Mikal—the catch in his breath that her kiss caused, the citrus smell of his after-shave, the smoothness of his cheek beneath her hand. She held him close, wanting more of him. "Colonel Hidalgo says...before daybreak I have to go."

Mikal swallowed hard, closed his eyes hard, felt hard, and knew this was insane. "The room they gave me is close by," he whispered into the soft comfort of her hair.

"Take me there."

## Chapter Ten

Morgan followed Mikal through the garden and down some tiled steps to a lower level of the terrace where another set of French doors opened to his room. He drew the drapes, throwing everything into pitch darkness. He gave her hand a quick squeeze before he released it, then fished a book of matches from the breast pocket of his jacket. He found his way to the bureau and extracted a match. Striking it, he located the candles he'd planted there earlier.

"Not enough light to draw any attention." When three candles were aflame, he tossed the matches aside and turned to Morgan. "But enough so I can see you."

"You have such a thing for candles."

He went to her, gathered her in his arms and turned her profile to the light. "I have such a thing for your face bathed in candlelight." His kiss was slow, controlled, tantalizing. He whispered, "Your face bathed in sunshine." Another slow kiss, another quiet bit of praise. "Your sweet face bathed in anything. Morgan, I have such thoughts."

Her stomach tightened and her knees grew weak. "Thoughts of what?"

"Thoughts of bathing you." His breath flowed hot against her neck. "But I can't run the water in the tub. Someone would hear."

"The pool outside..."

"Someone would see."

"...would be so nice. It's hot."

"Because you're wearing too many clothes."

Her dress was gathered at the neck, but when he released the string that held it, it slid past her shoulders easily. He kissed the curve of her collarbone. "Was it cold when you left home?"

"Yes," she whispered, trying to remember what cold was, what caused it. "Bone-chilling wind."

"Chilled these beautiful bones, did it?"

"Mmm-hmm." Her dress dropped to the floor, leaving her in a satin teddy.

"And you missed me?"

"My bones did," she managed. He admired the full length of what he'd uncovered, lovely Morgan in a small wisp of satin, and the light in his eyes became a heated glow. He covered her breasts with his hands, and she quivered inside.

"Where else did you miss me, Morgan?" His gentle coaxing hardened her nipples beneath the satin, and she whimpered. "Tell me," he urged.

"My breasts missed you."

He kissed her, letting his tongue drift between her lips. "Ah, Morgan, they did." One hand strayed lower, smoothed her flat belly and dropped between her thighs. "And here," he whispered thickly. "Did you miss me here?"

"Oh, Mikal..."

"Yes, you did."

"Mikal..."

"I'm going to bathe you with my tongue," he promised. "I could bathe you inside, Morgan, but I'm not prepared for you this time."

She put her arms around him and held herself against him, testing his need. "You're such a gentleman, Mikal Romanov," she told him in a voice hoarse with tenderness. "I prepared myself for you." She looked up with soft, bright eyes. "But I appreciate the thought."

"Sure?" She nodded. "No more thinking, then."

"No more," she whispered as she pushed his jacket back from his shoulders. "Have you missed me?"

He shed his jacket. "Let me show you." The metallic clink of his belt buckle was followed by the click of a snap. "Let me show you how many ways I've missed you."

He showed her a hundred ways, and she responded in a hundred more. She was as gentle as he was; she was as wild. She was so lost in passion she had no idea where she was. She hadn't surveyed the room, and she didn't care. There was a bed, and Mikal was with her. She'd found him, and now she joined with him, greedy for the part of him that could not be taken back once given. She believed that with her heart, and her mind condoned the belief for her heart's sake.

Later, when they lay together quietly, their bodies glistening in the candle glow, Mikal said, "This is the way I think I missed you most."

"Hot and sweaty?"

He gave a low chuckle. "When I saw you teaching that class in the school gym, the way you threw your whole heart into those exercises, I had fantastic fantasies of other ways to get you hot and sweaty."

"They worked." She tasted the salty sheen of his shoulder. "Both ways."

"I beg your pardon, ma'am, but there were at least seven ways that worked quite nicely." He braced himself on an elbow and trailed a finger along her arm. "Very, very nicely."

"It's amazing how long you were able to sustain that . . ."

"Optimum pulse rate," he filled in, grinning.

"And without much warm-up."

"Instant warm-up when I saw you on the terrace. As you see, there's no cool down."

"We can't open a window, can we?" He shook his head, and she pushed her hair away from her neck. "I should tie my hair up."

"Don't you dare." With splayed fingers he combed it back from her face and let it spill in dark swirls over the white bed sheets. "The way I missed you most is relaxed and sated with our lovemaking. You're a paradox, you know." He tickled his chin with a hank of her hair, then made a loop of it and rubbed it over his cheek. "You're beautiful with your hair up, very prim, very sensible, very much in charge, but a little distant. Just out of reach, as though you were guarding some part of you." He smiled. "Now I know what it is."

"What part am I guarding?"

"The passionate lioness with the long, flowing mane. You pin up your hair to keep her in check."

"I pin up my hair to keep it off my neck and out of my way," she insisted. "Coming to this island is the wildest thing I've ever done, and I came with my hair pinned up."

He chuckled as he stroked her hair back again. "The lioness came dressed as Miss Dove so she wouldn't scare anybody."

She glanced up with a quizzical frown. "Do I scare you?"

"Sometimes."

"Why?"

Tenderly he caressed her cheek with the back of his hand. "Such delicacy makes me feel awkward sometimes, afraid to touch. The flip side of that is your fierce passion. You won't release yourself to me completely, but there are times when I get the feeling you want to drain me thoroughly."

"I want to give you . . . satisfaction," she said carefully.

"Believe me, you do. But there's more to it than that, I think."

Morgan stiffened. "I'm not making any demands on you, Mikal. Let's just be good to each other now and part friends when the time comes."

"Part friends?" She'd stepped into a hornet's nest to be with him, and she talked about parting as friends? Mikal wondered when the woman would ever know herself.

"What I mean is that I don't expect..." With a sigh, she told herself to relax, and she reached to touch the tousled hair that fell over his forehead. "You think like a poet, Mikal. Dreams are your reality. You even talk like a poet—about making love, and about lionesses and paradoxes. That's just your normal, everyday way of *talking*."

"Is it bad?" he asked seriously.

She gave her hair a quick toss and laughed as she pulled him into her arms. "It's beautiful. It's magic. I love the way you talk, the way you put things. It's Mikal, no one but Mikal."

"Actually, Miguel called you a paradox. 'A fascinating woman,' he said." The curves of her back and her buttocks served as a playground slide for his hand. "I had to remind him that I'm bigger than he is."

"Who's Miguel?"

"Colonel Miguel Hidalgo." Mikal lay back on the pillow and cradled Morgan in his arm. "The man who's keeping us all alive right now."

"I thought the man in charge was General Castillo."

"Theoretically, he is. This coup was a party they held in his honor—supposedly. The general is a popular man, a grandfatherly type, whose instincts tell him to back down on this hostage thing and throw in with the West. Nobody liked the last regime much— they spent a lot of money they didn't have on stuff they didn't need, and the people stayed poor. So the Castillo faction came to power without a fight, and our State Department would recognize them with no problem, if he could just put a cork in Guerrero."

She'd heard the name before, and she knew it inspired genuine feelings of dread. "Who is this Guerrero, anyway?"

"He's Castillo's nephew and heir apparent. He's a user. He worked for the old regime, then jumped sides when it was convenient, and now he has the general's ear and a good deal of influence over what army they have here."

"This island seems too small to have much military power," Morgan observed. She'd seen automatic weapons, truckloads of soldiers, and wary civilians, but nothing resembling heavy artillery.

"Guerrero doesn't know that. He envisions himself as a cigar-chomping Caesar with a military empire. Thanks to Hidalgo's diplomacy and Castillo's popularity, the State Department is sitting on hold."

"And the hostages?"

"They're on hold, too. It's a tug-of-war with Guerrero on one side and Hidalgo opposite him. The hostages are the rope."

Morgan sighed. "Why don't we call in the marines?"

"Because then the rope breaks, Morgan." He lifted her chin and tilted his head for a look at her face. "You want the leathernecks instead of the silver tongue? No faith in me?"

"I don't understand exactly what you do, Mikal." And then she added quickly, "But I do understand that they're armed and you're not. That's scary."

"You'd feel better if I stuck a gun in my belt."

"Maybe one of those little derringers inside your boot."

He laughed, hugging her. "I don't own a pair of boots. Besides that, they search me quite thoroughly before they let me anywhere near Castillo, and I mean *quite* thoroughly."

"Oh, Mikal, this is crazy. The secretary of state should be down here taking care of this. They're not going to kill the secretary of state."

"They're not going to kill me, either."

She braced herself on his chest to launch her barrage. "How can you stop them, Mikal? With words? You're a poet. Who's going to retaliate if they knock off one dreamy poet with a head full of beautiful words?"

His chest rumbled as he laughed. "If they could see the look in your eyes, we'd all be on our way home tomorrow. My ultimate weapon—my lioness." He tucked a stray lock behind her ear, thinking how much he loved that fall of hair. "I want you right there beside me, purring like a harmless kitten, the next time I have a session with Castillo and company."

She tossed her hair again and smiled. "I'll show them balance of power."

"Right on."

"Cold war, détente, no holds barred—whatever they want, I'm ready."

"We'll rewrite *High Noon*."

"And I won't have to sit home twiddling my thumbs and waiting for—" their eyes met, and their smiles faded "—news." She closed her eyes and settled over him, resting her cheek against his chest. There was no music sweeter than his heartbeat.

"I'm not much of a poet, Morgan, but I'm a pretty fair novelist. A few people might care if I got 'knocked off' down here. Freedom International commands some respect, as well, so we've got *something* going for us."

"Something bigger than a derringer?"

"God, I hope so."

Hope springs eternal, she thought, especially in the mind of a dreamer. "What do you talk about in these sessions?"

"It depends. Castillo likes to talk about women, foreign aid, the price of pork and the CIA. Guerrero wants to impress me with his party line and his knowledge of weaponry, and Miguel wants to know what kind of school my son goes to and where he could get a grant to remodel the hospital here in La Primavera. Sometimes Miguel turns me loose in the kitchen and talks politics and philosophy while I cook us a decent meal."

"For heaven's sake, Mikal, what about the hostages?"

"That's what I choose to discuss, and the trick is in bringing them up whenever everyone's being reasonable. Miguel wants to let them go as a goodwill gesture. Castillo sees them as insurance."

"And Guerrero?"

Mikal sighed. "Guerrero is a fool." The truth was that Guerrero was a madman, but he chose not to use the word.

"He's willing to kill people," Morgan assumed.

He's *anxious* to kill people, Mikal amended silently, but aloud he offered hope. "Miguel Hidalgo is a reasonable man, though Guerrero's relationship to Castillo puts him in better standing with the old man. Miguel was educated in the States, and he knows what we have to offer. Right now, though, he has to play down his American sympathies, because independence fever is running pretty high."

"Then Castillo is just a pawn?"

Mikal shook his head. "I wouldn't say that. He's a wily old buzzard who's weighing his options."

It struck Morgan as an outrageous absurdity. A tiny island paradise, an uncontested coup and some men drunk with sudden power had the State Department "on hold," while innocent people waited to go home if sanity prevailed—or to be shot if it didn't. What messes these dreamers get themselves into, she thought, and the thought gave her a queasy feeling.

"Why are they holding my father?"

"Basically, I think it's because Guerrero doesn't like missionaries. I gather he had some experience with mission schools when he was a kid. Anyway he says your father was in thick with the old regime. He's holding a young teacher under the same pretense."

"And the others?"

"A reporter, two college kids supposedly suspected of drug possession, a doctor—and then there's the woman with the haunted eyes."

"Are you being poetic again?"

"Can't think of any other way to describe her," he said absently as he pictured her. She'd reminded him of a trapped animal. "The others are American, but I'm not sure about her. She won't talk. She's terrified of Guerrero."

"Is she pretty?"

"She's beautiful." He enjoyed Morgan's even, controlled stare for a moment before he gave way to a smile and allowed a twinkle to creep into his eyes. "But plain as a pilgrim next to you."

She kissed the middle of his chest, catching a bit of soft, curly hair between her lips for a playful tug. He only laughed. "Do you have any idea how beautiful you are, Mikal Romanov?"

"I'm dreamy," he reminded her. "You said so yourself."

"I meant that you're a dreamer. Purely insatiable, and I have a terrible weakness for your kind."

"Oh really?" He rolled with her in his arms, and she looked up at him. "I didn't think there were enough like me to make up a whole 'kind.'"

"Dreamers," she said with a sigh. "Idealists. If you've met my father, you know what I mean."

"I've met your father, and I admire him. Was there someone else who fell into that troublesome category?"

"It's not a matter of being troublesome. It's a matter of being impossible to live with." This was not the time for this discussion, she thought. All she wanted was to be close to Mikal for a few hours. She turned, settling her shoulders back, letting her attention drift to the shadowed ceiling. "There was Jeremy," she said quietly. "But we had sense enough to realize it wouldn't work."

"Your good sense has served you well. Artists can be such eccentrics." He caught her incredulous glance and grinned. "Really. You're much too sensible to get hooked up with some crazy artist."

"I certainly have taken leave of my senses, haven't I?"

"I wouldn't say so." He was thirsty, and the only thirst-quencher at hand was in the fruit bowl someone left for him each day. He reached behind him and located the bowl. "I'd say coming to this powder keg of an island is perfectly sane. I did it myself. Have a grape."

A bunch of purple fruit dangled above her nose. Morgan stretched her neck and captured a grape with her teeth. The skin burst and filled her mouth with sweet juice. She bobbed for a second one. "Delightful." She watched him put several into his own mouth before he offered her another chance. "Is this the forbidden fruit?"

Lips glistening with grape juice, Mikal offered a slow smile as he reached to the bowl, keeping his eyes on her. He came up with another offering. "This," he whispered suggestively, "is the forbidden fruit."

"What is it?" Morgan tested the smooth skin with her lips and found that it had more give than an apple. It felt cool, and she took a healthy bite. Sweet juice escaped the corner of her mouth.

"It's passion fruit." He swept up the errant dribble with his tongue. They shared the plumlike fruit, and when they were done, they shared the flavor that lingered on their lips.

"Do you have any idea how beautiful you are?" he asked.

"No. Tell me."

"Let me show you."

Morgan found herself standing before the mirror and she saw the reflection of three flickering candles and two nude people. One was tall, broad-chested and breathtakingly handsome, and in front of him was a dewy-eyed woman who looked so completely content with her natural state that Morgan hardly recognized herself. Her breasts peeked through a cascade of dark hair, her mouth was moist and puffy from his kisses, and her skin bore a satiny sheen.

Mikal moved the fall of hair behind one shoulder and cupped her breast in his hand. She gave his reflection a saucy smile. "What metaphor comes to mind? Grapes or passion fruit?"

He dipped his head to kiss her shoulder. "A flower," he murmured. "An orchid. So pretty. Such a soft, sweet petal here." She watched the mirror as though it were a movie screen, reminding herself that the sensations were real. "And here," he whispered, and she watched. The delicate caresses were being applied under her breast, over her belly, along her thigh, and her breathing became tremulous. "And here." Mikal lifted her hair and kissed the side of her neck and then the curve of her ear. "So pretty," he said again. "Open up for me, Morgan. Let me get deep inside you."

"You have." She gasped when he slid his hand from one thigh to the other, lingering momentarily at the intimate bridge between them. "Oh, Mikal, you will again."

"Only physically, unless you decide to trust me with more." He brought his hands to her shoulders. "Look at us, Morgan."

She did, and she giggled. "We're both stark naked."

"That's an honest observation. That's what the little boy in the crowd said when the emperor paraded through town in his imaginary clothes. The boy was a realist. I see naked people, too, but my mind's eye sees all kinds of other possibilities."

"That's what makes you a dreamer. I'm like the little boy. I say we're both stark naked." But beautiful, some part of her insisted. As ludicrous as the situation seemed when she put it in plain and simple terms—that they were standing nude in the middle of an armed camp of revolutionaries—they were beautiful, as was the moment. She found wonder in that fact.

"And I say I like us that way," he said, turning her in his arms. "But I also like the possibilities." He gave her a gentle kiss.

"What kind of possibilities?" she mumbled.

"The best kind, Morgan." He pressed the heels of his hands along the firm ridges of muscle in her back and soared on sensation when she swayed against him. "We have wonderful possibilities."

Morgan's head dropped back with the intensity of their next kiss. If it were possible to become one with him now, she knew she would be whole. Her senses short-circuited, sparked and crackled with the need to be connected to his. She rose on tiptoe, pressed herself against him, tightened her arms around him, and sent her tongue to meet his. Suddenly his lips weren't there anymore, and he clamped his hand over her mouth. Morgan reeled with the shock.

"Don't make a sound."

She struggled to make sense of the hot warning in her ear. His face, tight with tension, came into focus. Wide-eyed, she nodded.

Mikal licked his thumb and forefinger and snuffed the candles. Moving quickly and quietly, he stood Morgan in the corner of the room behind the heavy drapes and breathed one more warning in her ear. "Stand perfectly still."

She assumed that he returned to the bed, though she heard no sound. Probably, she realized, because her heart was pounding so loudly in her ears. She flattened herself against the wall, trying to become part of it. What had he heard? They'd been kissing, and she'd been aware of nothing but their erratic breathing. Now the staccato thump of her heart filled her ears and she thought her temples might burst.

A door opened. A light came on. A man voiced what sounded like a string of demands in Spanish. A second voice chimed in. Then Morgan recognized Mikal's sleepy, *"¿Qué pasa?"*

What was going on, indeed? It was one of the few Spanish phrases Morgan recognized. She heard other doors opening and closing, presumably the bathroom and the closets, while Mikal and the men conferred. A strange voice drew closer, and Morgan held her breath. She imagined herself being discovered, and she thought, *Oh, God, not stark naked!* Lowering only her eyes, she realized that the drapes allowed a smidgen of light to pass beneath them, which meant that even though she was standing on her toes, her heels braced against the wall, there might be a sliver of exposed flesh. She gripped the sill of the window with her right hand, and she prayed. Rivulets of sweat streamed down the sides of her face as she listened to a conversation she couldn't understand and hoped that her heart's drumroll couldn't be heard beyond the curtain.

Mikal's effect on the other two men was discernible even from behind the curtain. The demands became more civil as his tranquility prevailed. He sounded thoroughly unruffled, and the other voices became calmer.

*"Lo siento, señor."* The man was apparently satisfied, even apologetic.

*"No importa."*

The door closed and the room was dark again. Still, Morgan was unable to move. When Mikal drew the curtain back, she fell into his arms.

"This was crazy, Morgan. We've got to get you out of here."

His urgency scared her. "But Colonel Hidalgo brought me here, and he's one of the men in charge."

"Guerrero came along and found no sentries in this wing." He led her to the bed and found her clothes. "He stationed one, and the guy thought he heard something, so he brought the other one along to back him up."

"Do you think Hidalgo..."

"I think he'll meet us in the garden when he said he would, and you're going to wait for him there. The atrium is part of his suite. There's little chance of anyone snooping around. This is the only other room with access to the garden, and to get through here they'd have to get through me."

"Mikal..."

In the dark he caressed her cheek with a reassuring palm. "They *won't* get through me."

"But, Mikal..."

"Trust me." He kissed her softly.

"But can we trust Hidalgo?"

"We have to. If he double-crosses us, you're in here with the rest of us."

"Mikal, I want to see my father."

He was quiet for a long moment as he combed her hair back with his fingers and then cupped her cheek in his hand again. "Please don't try, Morgan. He's as well now as he would be if you saw him, and there's nothing you can do to help. The opposite, in fact. Please, go home."

She covered his hand with hers and tried to think sensibly. She tried to remember what practicality was. Her blood pounded in her ears, and all she could think of was that her father was there, and she loved him. Mikal was there, and she loved him, too. She turned her lips to his palm. "I'll call David and tell him I've seen you again," she whispered.

"Thank you."

She dressed quickly. He kissed her soundly, swallowing the lump in his throat that told him she would be gone from the island within hours, and whispered, *"Vaya con Dios, cara mia."*

Carrying her sandals, she slipped out into the night. The cool air was a blessing. Keeping to the shadows, she took the stone steps two at a time and found a hiding place in the garden where Mikal had waited just hours before. The candles in the shrine had gone out. Ears fully alert, she watched the atrium door.

Darkness obscured the identity of the man who came through the door sometime later, but he crossed the terrace with a purposeful stride. He clearly knew that she was there. Morgan stiffened where she stood behind the acacia.

"Miss Remark?" He reached the shrine and stopped, peering into the lush greenery. "It's Hidalgo. I heard what happened."

Relieved, Morgan stepped from behind the tree. "Why did they search his room like that?" she whispered. "Is Mikal a prisoner or not?"

Hidalgo sighed. "I'm hoping he's a bridge. I had told the sentry that I'd provided him with some, uh, distraction for the evening and that he was to turn a deaf ear. The man apparently decided to desert his post and find his own distraction." Hidalgo shook his head. "A young recruit with little training. He should be in school. With any luck, he soon will be."

In his jeans and cotton T-shirt, Hidalgo hardly looked the part of a military man himself. Mikal trusted him, and instinct told her that Mikal was right. They were birds of a feather, Morgan decided, two dreamers of the same kind.

"McQuade should be waiting for you outside the gate. I'll escort you past the guards. It will appear to them that you were...my companion this evening." Morgan nodded, and Hidalgo gestured toward the terrace.

They passed two uniformed men in the foyer, and Hidalgo hooked his arm around her shoulders. He mumbled something to her in Spanish, then laughed. She giggled, but her blush was real. The act was repeated twice more before they passed through the gates, crossed the street and strolled two blocks. They found McQuade, waiting under a street sign. As the two approached, he took one last pull of his cigarette and ground it beneath his heel.

"What are your plans now, Miss Remark?" Hidalgo asked. "Are you ready to go home?"

"Colonel . . . I have a confession to make."

McQuade's grip on her shoulder was less than gentle. "The colonel isn't a priest, Morgan, and this is no time for any revealing confessions."

Morgan shrugged away from McQuade's grasp as she searched Hidalgo's face for some sign of understanding. She decided she saw it in his eyes. "I'm not who I said I was, Colonel Hidalgo."

Miguel chuckled. "You're not Mikal Romanov's secretary?"

"No, I'm not. Mikal and I—"

"Morgan," McQuade warned.

"Your devotion to him is obvious, Miss Remark." Miguel offered McQuade a relaxed smile. "Do you think I'm blind, McQuade? I have a soft spot in my heart for romances such as theirs."

"My name is Morgan Kramer, Colonel. You're holding my father."

The smile dropped from Miguel's face. "You shouldn't have lied to me." He slid a cutting glance at McQuade. "Nor you."

McQuade shrugged. "I thought she'd be satisfied after a visit with Mikal and go home. Being Kramer's daughter shouldn't change anything. Nobody's threatening anybody here, or so you keep telling me.''

"Mikal is a guest. Reverend Kramer is...somewhat suspect.''

"You don't suspect him any more than I do," McQuade reminded him.

Miguel turned to Morgan again. "This is a delicate situation, Miss Re—Kramer. The fewer the complications, the better for all of us.''

"I want to see my father." She knew she sounded like a spoiled American, but at the moment she didn't care.

"It wouldn't be wise," Miguel told her.

The night crowded close around her, and feelings jostled in her brain. She had opened herself for Mikal, whether he knew it or not, and suddenly she was just a mass of feelings. Feelings she'd been harboring for a long time now had a name, and though she knew that loving Mikal was as foolish as loving her father, still, there it was.

"I haven't seen my father in years, Colonel, and he's my only family. I don't know what you people plan to do with him, but I'm here and I want to see him.''

"He'll be home soon. You can see him then.''

"Can you guarantee that?''

Miguel Hidalgo was nothing if not an honest man. "I'll do all I can.''

"I'm sure you will. He's an old man, Colonel. If all you can do isn't enough...and if Mikal's efforts fail..."

"Mikal has the general's ear. He's listening," Miguel assured her, "and I truly believe—"

"I want to see my father, Colonel."

## Chapter Eleven

General, the man's health is failing." There was no sense of urgency in Mikal's approach. The health of one aging missionary was not of major concern to General Castillo, but his international image was. "If you were to send Sidney Kramer home now, the gesture would be well received in Washington."

"It would be taken as a sign of weakness."

Guerrero's gravelly voice never failed to command attention. When he spoke, the natural lilt of the Spanish language became guttural. It was said that a boyhood injury to his throat had damaged his vocal chords, but that was only conjecture. Guerrero never offered any personal history. Mikal had heard two different stories about the four-inch scar that bracketed Guerrero's left eye and several explanations for the black pigskin gloves he always wore. Mikal was convinced that Guerrero had designed an image of villainy for himself and that he was more than a little melodramatic in dressing the part.

"I think we need to be realistic about our strengths and weaknesses, General," Miguel Hidalgo countered. "And I think we need to move toward establishing who we are now."

Mikal's relaxed posture was deceptive as he studied the three men who shared the table with him. In discussions with them, he was never relaxed. He chose every word carefully and analyzed every reaction. Guerrero sat to Castillo's left and Hidalgo to his right. Mikal wondered where Guerrero had gotten his medals. He knew about the man's participation in other Latin American insurrections, and he wondered whether the medals had been awarded or whether Guerrero had claimed them for himself. In either case, Mikal suspected that Guerrero slept in his uniform, complete with decorations.

Hidalgo, on the other hand, resisted such trappings. He wore the short-sleeved khaki uniform with its insignia of rank, but no medals, no epaulets or gold "scrambled egg" embroidery, rarely even a hat. Mikal suspected that Miguel was somewhat embarrassed by the pompous claims such finery would make for a colonel who had never been a captain. He knew that the general required the uniform, and Miguel deferred to the old man's wishes.

"I agree," Guerrero said, eyeing Hidalgo with disdain. "We are an independent Caribbean nation. Following Cuba's example, we must demonstrate that land mass and power are not synonymous."

Mikal checked mentally through his hand, looking for a card to play. "Sir, this man is a missionary, a man of the church. Not only that, he's old. The world will sympathize with him almost as it would with . . . a defenseless woman or child." The comparison fit the general's concepts, but Mikal almost choked on the "defenseless woman" part. Morgan's image came to mind with the very word *woman*, and the phrase became absurd. "You are a man who defends the defenseless, General. That's why your people look to you for leadership."

"The general's concern is for the fate of the many— men, women and children. The people of De Colores, Mr. Romanov," Guerrero said, as though he were rehearsing lines, "are the general's only concern."

"I have to be concerned about our image abroad, as well," the general said, settling his bulky body back in his chair. If his white beard had been longer and a bit fuller, Mikal thought, the general could have exchanged his khaki uniform for a red one at Christmastime. The general tried to placate Guerrero with a fatherly smile. "That's why I rely on the two of you to keep me centered. You are my muscle, and Miguel is my visionary. I am just an old farmer."

Mikal's smile came easily. "I have the greatest respect for old farmers. My father is one, as was his father. His feet are firmly planted in the earth, along with his wheat.''

''And you, I suspect, are his visionary.''

''He would be hard-pressed to find so kind a word. You, General Castillo, are the visionary. You understand the need for balance between muscle and compassion.''

''Yes, I do.'' The old man sighed as he checked his watch and then searched for the pills in his breast pocket. ''I need water, Miguel.'' Hidalgo pushed his chair back from the table, and the general continued. ''I tend toward the compassionate, myself, so I must defer almost entirely to my advisers for muscle. And I must weigh each move I make carefully. I cannot afford to think with my heart.'' He smiled sadly at Mikal as he tapped two fingers against his chest. ''It's tired and doesn't do its job so well.''

Miguel was back with a glass of water. ''You should rest now, General.''

''Ah, *siesta*.'' After swallowing his medicine with a long drink of water, the general wagged a finger at Mikal. ''You cannot construe my afternoon naps as weakness, Mikal Romanov. Not on this island. Here, *siesta* is part of the good life.''

''I know that, sir.'' Mikal stood in deference to the older man, who used the arms of his chair for leverage as he came to his feet. ''The easygoing attitude here is just my style. I'm thinking of taking up permanent residence.''

''Who knows?'' the general responded, his eyes twinkling. ''Maybe you already have.''

Mikal returned to his room, dreading the prospect of meeting with Yuri and the others that afternoon. He knew that if he could meet with Castillo without Guerrero's presence, the old man would agree to a release of all detainees. Morgan had the idea that weapons made the difference, but Mikal had been at this long enough to know that wasn't true. Guns would not gain him any friends, nor would ten armed men keep him safe. Being unarmed didn't scare him. Guerrero was a man who was incapable of reasoning, and it was that fact alone that was frightening.

A blast of heat rose from the tiled terrace when Mikal opened the French doors. Leaving the confines of his room, he headed for the coolness of the garden. He took the steps three at a time. At the higher level he found a breeze that made the afternoon air a little less heavy. He was a man of the high plains. Humidity drained his energy, and he had to fight to keep it from draining his spirits.

Mikal noticed the remains of the candles he'd burned four nights ago at the little wooden shrine. Shoving his hands in his pockets, he let his head drop back, closed his eyes and smelled the garden scents, the passionflower and the acacia. He teased himself with the idea of opening his eyes and seeing Morgan.

"She's still here, you know."

Mikal turned sharply and found that Miguel had sought the solitude of the garden in advance of him. Mikal joined him on the wrought-iron bench in a shady spot near the pool. The two men had a tacit agreement to speak English when they were alone.

"Since you hadn't told me otherwise, I thought she probably was."

"She wants to see her father."

Mikal was surprised. Until now Miguel hadn't mentioned his knowledge of Morgan's identity. "She can't come here again, Miguel. It's too risky."

"I'm inclined to arrange it for her at this point."

"Why?"

Miguel lit a cigarette and watched as a gray cloud of smoke floated toward the palms. "Castillo is just what he says—a farmer turned revolutionary. And I'm a teacher turned revolutionary."

This would have something to do with Morgan's request. It was Mikal's genius to know that, and to wait for the man to come to the point, however long it took. In the process, he would learn more about the men who held those whom Mikal had come to regard as *his* people.

"I hadn't figured you for a teacher."

Meeting Mikal's smile with a shrug, Miguel began, "There have been few fortunes made on this island, but my father was one who made his. He lives in Switzerland now. Our lives contrasted sharply with those of most of the islanders, who are generally poor. I was educated at the University of Massachusetts, taught there for two years, and then came home. I became a teacher, then an agitator, and finally a revolutionary." He chuckled with the memory. "Those in power were fat and complacent, and the plum was ripe for picking. It fell into our hands. Guerrero was hoping for more resistance."

"And what was Guerrero before he became a revolutionary?" Mikal wondered.

"Guerrero isn't a revolutionary," Miguel said quietly. "He is a brawler who's found the niche of his dreams. He is suddenly a hero, and he has the army in his pocket. If Castillo were not father, grandfather, or godfather to half the people on this island..." Shaking his head, he returned his cigarette to his mouth and puffed angrily. "Castillo was the grandfather, and I was the teacher. In the evenings we would sip rum and plan all the improvements we would make. When the opportunity presented itself, we took it."

"With the help of your friend with the muscle."

"That's right. Castillo's nephew."

How much will he tell me? Mikal wondered. How far can we go with this? "One or the other of you will succeed him," he mused. "Are you ready for that?"

"I'm a teacher." Miguel's tone was flat, and his stare was empty of expression.

"And Guerrero is... a brawler? I think that's an understatement."

Miguel was quiet, reflective. "I need time."

"How big is the army?"

Miguel looked at Mikal and smiled as his attention focused again on the present. "I would be a traitor if I told you that, my friend. But you didn't expect me to, did you?" Mikal offered a lopsided grin, and Miguel laughed. "You are a master, Mikal. I would promise you a job in my government, but when we become a quiet little tourist spot again, there will be little need for your talents."

"My talents run to writing, Miguel. Maybe I could write travel brochures."

They laughed together now, trading fantasies. "We'll let you review our restaurants, if you won't be too critical."

"Maybe I could open my own—Mikal's Place."

"Miguel's," Miguel corrected. "We have the same name."

The same name, Mikal thought, but worlds apart. Mikal would soon return to the Midwest, where he would once again be the eccentric writer down the block who was always speaking up about some cause or other. Miguel faced a day of reckoning here, and no one could predict when that day might come.

"Then help me, Miguel, for the sake of—" Mikal opened his hands in a beckoning gesture "—our common name. Help me get these people home."

Miguel's gaze strayed to the pool as he took one last drag on his cigarette before crushing it beneath his shoe. "Kramer is ill, Mikal. You know that."

"That's why it's important that we start with him."

"I find it hard to refuse to let a daughter visit a father who is not well."

Mikal drew a long, slow breath. "I do, too."

"I'm not in a position to make any promises about the detainees, Mikal, but I can bar her from the palace if that's what you want."

He wanted her to go home, he reminded himself. He wanted to go home with her. He wanted to crawl under a blanket with her and listen to the North Dakota wind howl outside his window. He wanted to see her.

"Can you keep her clear of Guerrero?"

"I can try."

Morgan followed Miguel down the corridor she knew led to Mikal's room. She had been warned that her father was not well and that her visit would be brief, but she had some ideas of her own on that score. She had dressed in a loose, black, gauze dress and covered her hair with a lace mantilla, as she'd been instructed to do. She looked like a nondescript nocturnal visitor, but she'd decided that if her father's condition warranted it, she could become something more. A smaller voice reminded her that she hadn't decided what.

Mikal was waiting for her.

"I'll go ahead of you and clear the way," Miguel instructed, pointedly eyeing first one American, then the other. Mikal and Morgan had eyes only for each other, and Miguel wondered whether he would have to remind them that this was not the time. "Ten minutes, Mikal, and then bring her back here. I'll expect her to be out of there by—" he checked his watch "—nine-thirty. The guard will be back at his post by then. Pay close attention to the time."

With three fingers he told them to give him as many minutes to prepare the way, and then he closed the door softly behind him.

Mikal laid a hand on Morgan's shoulder, and she swayed, turned and let him steady her in his arms. "I should be angry with you," she told him as her arms surrounded his waist.

"Why?" he whispered into her hair.

"You didn't tell me he was ill."

"High blood pressure. You knew that, didn't you?"
She shook her head.

"Dr. Kelsch, one of the other hostages, has kept
close watch on him, but this whole ordeal has taken its
toll."

The slow, soothing circles his hands made over her
back told her that he knew the full extent of the toll it
was taking on her. "Does he know I'm here?" she
asked.

"I told him you'd gotten some help from Freedom
International and the Red Cross. I didn't tell him
about the risk you're taking."

It seemed ridiculous, she knew, after all the years of
little communication between them, but it was important that she see her father now. In fact, if she
could take him to safety, she thought she could be at
peace with him. It occurred to her that the world's
practical people had a duty to look after dreamers,
whose heads had gotten so far into the clouds that
their enemies had a clear shot at them.

"I just need to see him," she said.

"Yes, I know. And it's time."

They walked together along a hallway, down a flight
of steps and through another hallway. Responding to
some instinct for defense, Morgan took note of
everything—the wrought-iron sconces and colorful
woven wall hangings, the red tile, the white walls, and
the absence of any sign of people. If she needed to, she

would know her way out, she thought as she ventured deeper into the heart of the palace.

They passed through an anteroom, where Mikal told her at least two guards usually stood watch, often over a hand of cards or a game of checkers. Though the room was temporarily vacant, Mikal knew there would be guards at either end of the corridor. He tried the handle of a heavy wooden door and was half surprised to find it open. He motioned for Morgan to follow him.

The large room was dimly lit by a corner lamp. Furniture and other trappings faded out of focus for Morgan as Mikal hurried her past several people, all men, all staring vacantly as she passed. Her presence posed no threat, offered no promise. They sat in chairs or on pallets spread over the floor. The fourth face she saw she recognized. Yuri! He smiled, and she opened her mouth to speak, but Mikal tightened his grip on her arm. "Quickly, Morgan. Through here."

The room was small, but the open window allowed the evening breeze to keep the air comfortable and fresh. In the shadows a man sat on a bed, waiting.

"Morgan."

At the sound of her name, Mikal's hand eased away from her, but she caught his arm, wordlessly asking him not to go far.

"They tell me you've been ill," she said quietly. She fought the urge to be a little girl again, to give him a joyous hug.

"Not so ill that I couldn't handle a kiss."

His voice seemed only slightly less than pulpit strong, which Morgan found encouraging. She had once imagined that even if his whole body disintegrated like the Cheshire cat's, his voice would still be there. She sat beside him on the bed and gave him a peck on the cheek, while Mikal stood watch near the door. It was strange to find that her father was gray and frail rather than robust and hearty, as he had been when she'd last seen him—how many years ago? So little time, she thought. So much to say.

"Mikal will make them listen, Father. I know he will."

At his post, Mikal smiled to himself. When had she decided that? he wondered.

"Mikal and Yuri are good men," Sidney Kramer remarked as he patted Morgan's hand, "but they risk too much by being here, and so do you."

"I think it's some game these people are playing," Morgan offered. "I don't think they mean to harm anyone."

"Neither do I." They sat in silence for a moment before he asked, "What made you come?"

"I couldn't get a straight answer from anyone," she said. *And you were here. And so was Mikal.* But she didn't dare suggest such a foolish reason aloud.

"So you came looking for the answers yourself. You were always one to take charge."

Her father's small chuckle sounded hollow. It was unlike the deep, resounding laugh she'd always associated with him; this one issued from his throat rather than his chest. "How are you feeling...really?"

"Better now that I've seen you, Morgan, but when I know you're safe, I'll be just fine."

"By this time tomorrow she'll be stateside." With a shoulder braced against the doorjamb, Mikal cast her a pointed look. "Right, Morgan?"

"My father should be in a hospital, Mikal."

"He will be, just as soon as I can manage it. Right now—" Mikal tilted the face of his watch toward the light "—you've got one minute."

"Is there anything you need? The Red Cross can surely see that . . ." Morgan touched her father's arm. "Do you have medication?"

The old man nodded. "Our basic needs are taken care of. I need prayers."

Morgan's chin dropped in deference to the suggestion he'd offered ever since she could remember. It was a reminder that traditionally brought a twinge of guilt, because she'd usually been too anxious to get the job done on her own to remember her father's training. "Of course," she said quietly.

Sidney Kramer lifted his daughter's chin in his hand, and she looked up at him. "I need your forgiveness."

Morgan was shaken by the simplicity of the words and the enormity of their meaning. "You did what you had to do with your life," she said. "But I've missed you."

"Thank you for coming here to tell me that."

She hugged his neck briefly, feeling awkward, but also relieved, and she responded to Mikal's quiet reminder by pulling herself away abruptly. "You'll come to Bismarck when they release you?"

Her father lay down almost as soon as Morgan had given him the room to do so. "Yes," he said. "Now go with Mikal. We don't want to press our luck by running over their time limit. Take care, Morgan."

Morgan moved past Mikal as she left the room. She heard her father call Mikal back, and the weakening sound of his voice alarmed her. But it was Mikal he'd called, and Morgan stood rooted to the spot. Within moments Mikal reappeared at the door and signaled for Dr. Kelsch, who hurried to the minister's bedside.

"What's wrong?"

Mikal's expression was tightly fixed. "Nothing new. We have to get you out of here, Morgan."

"I want to know what's wrong." A door opened at the other side of the hostages' common room, and from the corner of her eye Morgan noted the faces of first one woman, then another. They didn't concern her. It was her father's need for the doctor that worried her, but Mikal was pushing her toward the big wooden door, where Yuri stood, listening. She jerked her arm away. "Mikal!"

"Your father is as stubborn as you are," Mikal barked; then he remembered himself and lowered his voice. "He doesn't want to be released without the others. He thinks his condition brings some pressure to bear, and it sure as hell does. On *me*. Because he's sick, and because he's *your* father, and because you're—" He snatched her arm again and propelled her toward the door. "You're going home, and he's next. Then maybe we can get something done here."

"He called you. You called for the doctor. I want to know why," she demanded, struggling.

"Mikal!" Yuri motioned them back as he inclined his head toward the door.

Mikal closed his eyes briefly as he pulled Morgan back against him and muttered, "What the hell am I going to do with you now?" But in an instant he moved in the direction of the room where the women slept. "Stay here," he ordered, and closed the door.

Morgan stared dumbfounded at the two women whose faces she'd glimpsed only briefly before, and they stared back. A blonde with a short, pert hairstyle stood by the room's only window. She'd apparently just closed the blinds. From Mikal's description Morgan recognized the slender young woman who sat on the bed as the beauty with the haunted eyes. One long, dark braid was hitched over her shoulder, and her eyes, startlingly blue, were sunken and underscored with dark circles.

"You're Mr. Kramer's daughter?" the blonde asked. Morgan nodded, thinking there probably wasn't time for a chat. "I'm Judy, and this is Elizabeth. And you're crazy to sneak in here like this."

"So I'm told."

"Dr. Kelsch agreed to come here because one of the college kids got his shoulder dislocated when they arrested him," Judy reported, "and they never let him go."

"Why do you think they're continuing to hold you?" Morgan asked as she took inventory of the room. She could hear voices on the other side of the door.

"Some kind of politics."

"Guerrero's madness."

Elizabeth's voice was surprising. She had a slight accent, much like Hidalgo's, and though her tone was flat with despair, there was a rich depth to it. Morgan was intrigued by the woman. "Are you—"

Judy interrupted. "I don't know where you can hide in here, but we'd better think of something in case—"

"Stand behind the door, Miss Kramer." Elizabeth stood and indicated a spot between the door and a tall bureau. "Judy and I are curious about the commotion out there. They'll see an empty room behind us."

From her risky hiding place, Morgan peeped over a door hinge to see three soldiers who were talking with Mikal in Spanish. A fourth followed the two colonels, Hidalgo and Guerrero, into the room. Guerrero was barking angrily, while Hidalgo spoke calmly, apparently asking questions. Mikal directed his comments to Hidalgo.

"Mikal insists that Mr. Kramer must be moved to a hospital at once," Elizabeth translated, ostensibly for Judy's sake. "He says that Dr. Kelsch can't stabilize his condition unless he can get him to a proper medical facility."

The discussion continued. Although Morgan understood none of the words, she saw that the power of Mikal's will had a visible effect on Guerrero's expression. That will needed no translation. The look in Mikal's eyes brooked no argument, and his stance was completely confident. At this critical moment, when a choice had to be made, Guerrero's bluster held no sway over Mikal's incontrovertible conviction. Hidalgo quietly dispatched two soldiers, who returned shortly with a litter. Morgan watched while her father was taken away.

Mikal followed Dr. Kelsch, and the whole contingency of captors trooped out with them, leaving Morgan behind with the captives. Yuri came to the door of the women's room as Morgan crept out from behind it.

"There's a good chance Mikal will be able to get them to fly your father to Miami now that they've allowed him to be hospitalized," Yuri said. "Obviously they don't want a corpse on their hands. That's a good sign."

Morgan shuddered. It wouldn't be just any corpse. "How can we get word on his condition?"

"If we get word, it will have to be through Mikal. He's become quite friendly with Hidalgo." Seeing her fear, Yuri gave Morgan's shoulder a comforting squeeze. "Stay in this room for now. The guards come and go in the common room, but they rarely bother the women. I think they're not so sure of Elizabeth's position here." He smiled at the other woman, who lowered her eyes without comment. "Mikal will come up with something."

It was nearly an hour before Mikal returned. In the meantime Morgan learned that Judy was a teacher.

She'd been arrested following the coup because she was an American employed by the former regime and she was suspected of collusion. Judy explained that one of the other men was a reporter who had been vacationing on the island when the coup took place. There were also two college students being held because one of them had had a small amount of marijuana in his possession when they were searched by the police.

"They offered to let Elizabeth go, but she wouldn't take them up on it." Morgan turned a questioning glance at the dark-haired woman, but Elizabeth only stared down at the hands in her lap. "They won't let her take her baby," Judy added quietly.

"Why not? What kind of—"

"Guerrero is his father."

Elizabeth's bombshell was allowed to reverberate for a moment and then lie quietly. Morgan couldn't bring herself to ask any of the obvious questions. A rap on the door broke the silence.

"It's Mikal," his voice announced through the door. Judy hastened to admit him, and then she and Elizabeth left the room.

Mikal closed the door and leaned back against it. "He'll be flown to Miami with Dr. Kelsch as soon as it's safe for him to make the trip."

An overwhelming sense of relief washed over Morgan. Her father would get the care he needed and, as a blessed bonus, he would be safely away from the island. Relief gave way to concern as she looked at Mikal, searching his face for some sign of triumph and finding none. She'd watched him from her hiding place, and she'd seen the essence of his strength. Now she saw his fatigue. One of his worries had been taken care of, but one still stood before him. She went over and took him in her arms as she laid her head against his chest.

"Thank you, Mikal." He stroked her long hair, planted a kiss in its center part and said nothing. She was a burden to him now; she knew that. "When I heard he was ill, I was afraid if I didn't come, I might not see him again. It was a selfish move on my part."

"And selfish of me to allow it," he reflected. "I wanted to see you, even for ten minutes. Even for two."

Leaning back, she held his face in her hands and smiled through gathering tears. "Isn't it silly? The chance of seeing you keeps me here on this godforsaken island. When I think about going back while you're still here . . ." She shook her head, because she didn't have the words to banish the sensible thought. She hardly knew herself anymore.

"It's foolish to try to be together here."

Her laugh, however small, was incongruent with the tear that spilled to her cheek. "It looks as though you're stuck with me now, though, doesn't it?"

He took the tear in the palm of his hand and swept it to her temple, lacing his fingers into the soft hair he loved. "I'll get you out of here, Morgan. I swear I will." Gripping a handful of hair, he lowered his mouth to hers, pressing hard, piercing the space between her lips, revealing the only personal need he'd felt compelled to satisfy in recent weeks—his need for her. It took monumental effort to get a grip on her shoulders and pull back.

"I have a meeting with the general. I think we've made some headway, and I want to press the advantage." Mikal traced Morgan's hairline with his fingers, while he savored the beauty of her face, committing each feature to memory. "Miguel maneuvered some slack time between guard shifts to get you in here. Now I want you to borrow Elizabeth's dress, put it over your own and wear that black mantilla. I think we can pass you off as her. She's allowed to see her baby sometimes, so that's what I'm going to suggest to Miguel."

He smiled and kissed her softly. "Stay in this room until Miguel gives the word." Another kiss, longer and even more gentle. "And light a candle for me," he whispered. Then he was gone.

Morgan changed, and then she waited for what seemed like an interminable length of time, chafing and sweating in a double layer of clothes. Judy chattered, while Elizabeth retreated to a corner and offered little comment. When Yuri came to the door, Morgan jumped at the opportunity to move on, however risky the move might be.

Miguel, dressed in his uniform, was waiting in the common room with more instructions. "The guards are seated to the right. You will stay on my left side, and we'll cross the room quickly, while Yuri talks to the soldiers. Keep your head down and this—" he indicated the lacy mantilla "—pulled around your face."

"The talks—" Yuri began.

"The talks are over." Miguel jerked his chin toward Morgan. "This one is my concern right now. If she's discovered, it's a new ball game, all new rules." He turned to Morgan. "When I speak to you in Spanish, just nod."

Morgan gauged her pace by Miguel's, nodding after what sounded like a question and keeping her eyes riveted to the floor. She was aware of Yuri's presence and his halting words to the guards in bad Spanish. As she neared the anteroom door, she reminded herself not to rush her exit, which she felt a sudden drive to do. Just five more steps, three more...

They retraced the route through the darkened hallways, stopping only once at an alcove, where Morgan stripped off Elizabeth's dress and stuffed it behind a small table. Miguel made a mental note to retrieve the dress as soon as he deposited Morgan with McQuade. Morgan hesitated at the door to Mikal's room, but Miguel told her, "He's not there. When we pass anyone, I'll be telling you I don't have time for you tonight, and you have to go home. You should look...disgruntled."

Morgan pulled her mantilla close around her face and managed the role with considerable flair. The news about the talks being over sounded discouraging, and she let real anger take her through her performance.

McQuade was waiting for her on the same street corner as before. He was wearing a familiar rumpled khaki bush jacket, and she wondered if he were smoking the same cigarette. A wild notion flashed through her mind that perhaps some projectionist was rerunning a film that she'd somehow gotten herself mixed up in. She stood back and watched as McQuade offered Hidalgo a cigarette. Smoke curled above their heads, and she wanted to suggest that they break for lunch. Perhaps they could have Mikal's quiche, if these two were sufficiently secure in their masculinity to try it. Why were these two men huddled on the street corner, while Mikal, a man whose design for living was entirely peaceful, was facing armed lions in their den? The absurdity incensed her.

"What will you do now?" she demanded. The two men turned to her, Hidalgo with a frown, McQuade raising one eyebrow as he smoked. "My father and Dr. Kelsch are out, and now the talks are over. Why? What's going to happen to the other seven people in there?"

"Understand that only five of those people were detained by our government," Miguel pointed out. "The other two asked to be here."

"Mikal is a prisoner in there and you know—"

"Wait a minute," McQuade injected, halting Morgan's accusations with a wave of his hand. "What do you mean, the talks are over? I got word about Kramer and Kelsch, but I was told... What's going on with the others?"

"Mikal was in excellent form this evening," Miguel reported, assuming an official posture. "The general was moved when Mr. Kramer's health obviously took a turn for the worse, partly because the general himself—"

"Yeah, yeah, come on, Miguel. What's going on?"

"Your State Department will be notified that the charges pending against all detainees have been dropped, and that Yuri Romanov will accompany them by plane to Miami tomorrow."

"What about Mikal?" Morgan and McQuade chimed almost simultaneously.

Miguel took a final drag on his cigarette, dropped it to the sidewalk and ground it beneath his heel. Expelling the smoke with a sigh, he reverted from official to friend. "Mikal will stay with us until we're satisfied—until *Guerrero* is satisfied—that the threat of foreign intervention is no longer a factor."

"Stay with you!" McQuade shot back. "What the hell does that mean?"

"It means that Mikal Romanov has negotiated a trade."

## Chapter Twelve

Mikal's accommodations had been changed. He'd returned to the common room to discuss the plans for the release with Yuri, but it was clear that when the others left, he would go no further than the anteroom. The area of the palace he was now in was the easiest to secure.

He'd known he didn't have much to trade. Although Castillo refused to call anyone a hostage, Mikal had pointed out that, should the need for a hostage arise, it ought to be someone the world might want back—someone like a novelist of some renown, someone important to an organization like Freedom International, whose Nobel Prize he mentioned more than once. A couple of college kids and a reporter would hardly be missed. More releases could only boost the new government's image, he'd said. As soon as De Colores had reestablished its diplomatic relations with the U.S., he would expect to be on his way.

Yuri had been in closer contact with the detainees than Mikal had, and he was chosen to explain the conditions of the release to Elizabeth. Mikal rose from his chair when Yuri emerged from the women's room with Elizabeth and Judy behind him.

"Elizabeth agrees," Yuri said.

"I'm sorry, Elizabeth," Mikal offered, seeking contact with her downcast eyes. "They said it had to be all of you or none, and there was nothing I could do about your son. Guerrero was..."

"I know," she said, almost inaudibly. Then her voice gained strength. "Guerrero is Guerrero."

"Maybe when this situation stabilizes..."

"Contempt for him will grow," she predicted. "He won't always have this power. I'll come back for my son."

"And I'll come back for you," Yuri promised Mikal, glancing behind him at the pair of soldiers who had come to escort the group to the next checkout point.

"Give me a few days, Uncle Yuri. Miguel's behind me, and Castillo's tired of the whole thing. I think I can finish this up without an incident."

Yuri shook Mikal's hand, and since that wasn't enough, he gave him one of his burly bear hugs. His pride in Mikal had the old man fairly bursting at the seams. Despite the unexpected complication Morgan had introduced, Mikal had done a wonderful job. As Yuri saw it, delaying Mikal now was just a face-saving gesture on Guerrero's part. Just a little hitch. Mikal would be home soon.

"I don't know where Morgan is."

Yuri leaned back and read the worry in Mikal's eyes. "Miguel will keep you posted. I'm sure she—"

"I haven't seen Miguel this morning. I don't know for sure what happened to her after she left here. She thinks she can just waltz in and out of this place whenever she... Check on her if you can, okay?"

Yuri nodded. Mikal needed a woman like his own Helen, Yuri thought. One who would stay put while Mikal did the work he was meant to do. "I expect that McQuade has gotten her into the hospital to see her father," he suggested.

"With any luck they'll be flying out on the same plane. You'll call David as soon as—"

"As soon as I get to a phone, Mikal. And there won't be a sound in this palace we won't hear," Yuri promised. "We have many ears."

Mikal stood to the side and watched as the doors were opened and "his people" were ushered from their prison. They looked anxious, unsure that freedom was really theirs for the taking. Too quickly the doors were closed behind them, and, despite the warm weather, Mikal felt cold.

* * *

"You won't be able to get in to see him, Morgan. Miguel won't help you, and neither will I, so be grateful for the arrangements we've managed to make, and get the hell out of here."

McQuade leaned across his desk and gave her his darkest scowl. Even Morgan was intimidated. She turned away, shrugging helplessly. She was frustrated with the constraints of the tiny office. She wanted to pace. "He's being deserted," she protested. "Even if I could just see Miguel, get some assurance from him..."

"Who do you think you are, Miss Kramer? Some ambassador, for God's sake? I'll see Hidalgo, I'll get some assurance, and *I'll* stick around until they let Mike go." He moved to her side of the desk, giving himself a moment to reform his thoughts. She wouldn't take kindly to the words that kept popping into his head, and if he didn't get this woman on the next plane out, he'd be stuck with her. And could she come up with schemes! He managed a smile. "He isn't being deserted, Morgan. He's got me."

"Humph. You think *you're* some ambassador or something? You're the reason I had to come down here in the first place," she grumbled as she allowed him to usher her out the door. "If you had kept the line of communication open, McQuade..."

"Yeah, I know. Now, remember, you're with Freedom International. You're accompanying Mr. Kramer back to Miami."

"What do you do for a living, McQuade?"

McQuade squinted as they stepped into the sunlight. "I'm a guardian angel."

Morgan flew to Miami with her father. His hospital stay there would last several days, and Morgan decided to stay with him. In her years with the school system, she had used very little of her leave, and now was the time to take advantage of it. She called David each evening. McQuade called Morgan to report that he had seen Mikal. Things were going well, he said.

Things were going well, she reminded herself. After three days of good medical care, her father looked much better. Already he was talking about a little mission church that might need him on an Indian reservation. He'd forgotten his promise to return to Bismarck. He would work until he dropped, Morgan realized, and nothing she could say or do would change that. She'd been at his bedside for three days, and she'd been learning about him.

"Why did you ever marry?" she wondered. There was no hostility in her voice. She was simply curious.

"I loved your mother," he answered just as simply.

"But not enough."

"How much is enough?" He covered her hand with his. There were things he would have managed differently if he could have, but he knew his life was as it was, and he had never felt it was his to do with as he pleased. "I loved your mother, and she loved me. We had one dream when we started out, but in later years, when you were older and needed more...more practical things, she said...well, she was right. She had to make a choice."

"Between you and me?"

"No, Morgan, between Bismarck and—what was it at the time? Kenya, wasn't it?"

"Then you made a choice, too," Morgan said.

Sidney Kramer shook his head. "My choice had been made for me long before that. I was who I was, what I had to give."

There was little left for me, she thought. And for her mother... "She died loving you, you know."

"Yes, I know. We were never without love for each other, Morgan. There came a time when we couldn't live in the same place, but there was never a question of not loving each other."

It was a strange arrangement, Morgan decided, and certainly not one she wanted for herself. Perhaps Mikal's choices had been made for him, too. She had seen who Mikal was and what he had to give. Loving him for what he'd already given her, she would wait for his release, and she would be there when he set foot on safe soil. She would be there to see for herself that he was truly home. But Morgan knew she couldn't live as her mother had. The relief she longed to experience in being able to touch him again would only be temporary, and that wasn't enough for her. There would be more missions and greater risks. Mikal would go where he was needed, do what he did so well.

And Morgan would quietly withdraw from the fringes of his dreams. They were too big for her.

The Miami airport was full of white suits and white dresses. There were the crisp, white, nautical uniforms of cruise line employees waiting for "snowbirds" to fly in from points north. There were chic white linens and crumpled white cottons, long sleeves pushed up to elbows, and jackets with bright white T-shirts underneath. Morgan stood near the gate, because she was impatient with sitting, and she watched the bustle of people. Every few minutes she glanced up at the clock. The plane was late, but Mikal was on his way home.

The plane's arrival from Mexico City was announced, and Morgan saw that Yuri and Freedom International attorney Alex Steiger, who'd been deeply involved in a discussion for almost an hour, were moving toward the door. There was a man from the State Department there, too, but he seemed content to stay out of the way for the moment. Two television cameramen took their places, while several reporters jostled for position. Morgan stood back, wondering whether she'd even have a chance to say hello.

McQuade came through the door first, and Mikal followed. The reporters started right in.

"Were you held on the island against your will, Mr. Romanov?"

"Were there any demands?"

"Were the demands met?"

"Were you traded for the group they released last week?"

Mikal smiled and promised a statement later as he scanned the crowd. Yuri shouldered past reporters, slapped McQuade on the back and hugged Mikal, while Alex followed with handshakes. But Mikal continued to search.

"Is she here, Uncle Yuri? I thought you said she was still . . ."

He saw her at last, standing alone, dressed in a light blue blouse and white tailored suit, her hair primly bound up at the back of her head. He wanted no one else but her. He wanted to drive this crowd back before he went to her, because he wanted no intrusions. He wanted to be home, and he saw home, sky blue and snowy white, waiting quietly by herself.

McQuade gripped Mikal's shoulder and muttered, "I'll run interference with the press." Mikal nodded.

"Mikal—"

"I'll talk to them all later, Uncle Yuri." Handing Yuri his bag, he added, "Communiqués and dirty socks. You and Alex sort them out."

Morgan's heart soared when Mikal stepped away from all the others and came to her. She felt too much just then, and there were too many people there. Her vision clouded as she clutched her purse tightly and smiled. "Mikal" was all she managed to say.

He put his hand at the top of her arm, then slid it down to hold her hand discreetly between them as he guided her down the concourse. He'd seen the promise of glad tears, and he didn't want to share them with anyone. "Hold that thought until we get into the cab," he said. "How fast can you walk?"

"As fast as you can."

The afternoon daylight was waning. They commandeered a cab and fell into each other's arms as soon as the door was closed. Unconscious of the man at the wheel, the meter, or the motion of the car, they shared a kiss. In the middle of it, Morgan heard the man's voice, but took no interest in what he said. Her mind was absorbed in the taste of Mikal's mouth.

It was Mikal who drew back into reality first. "Where are we staying?"

"Where? Oh . . . the Marriott."

"You have a room for me?"

She closed her eyes, nuzzled his neck, and whispered, "I have a room."

When they arrived Mikal used Morgan's phone and put in a call to his son. The sound of David's voice superseded all third- and fourth-hand messages. Mikal knew he'd have to answer a thousand questions before he left Miami, but his son's single question came first. The answer: he would be home the following night.

For now Mikal was safe. Morgan had waited for him. There were no other questions. He drew the drapes and tossed his jacket on a chair. Morgan hung hers on a hanger with her skirt, then kicked off her shoes and lined them up neatly with the sandals that were already there. When she turned, Mikal was beside her, already stripped down to his briefs. Morgan saw the pile of his clothes on the chair. Indeed there were no questions.

"Whenever I felt the urge to lose my cool, I planned this moment," he told her. "I've been over it in my mind a hundred times in the last few days. I'm giving you a shower first." Smiling, because the fantasy was so close to becoming a reality, he unbuttoned her soft blue blouse. "And I don't give a damn who hears the water running."

"Do I need a shower?" she asked innocently.

"I do, and I'm not letting you out of my sight while I take one." She let him slip the blouse off, but she caught it and hung it up when he would have dropped it to the floor. "That wasn't part of my plan," he teased. "I saw a trail of clothes."

"Okay." She swept her slip over her head. "Let the fantasy start now." The slip fell to the floor, along with their last articles of clothing. The next part of the plan was a long, hot kiss, followed by a long, hot shower.

They made each other clean with loving caresses given by soap-filled hands. They tasted each other, tested each other. They drove one another to the brink, then stood poised under the warm water, every nerve tingling as they consented to another brief retreat from fulfillment.

They came out of the shower and dried each other with thick towels. He took her wet hair down and dried that, too. But when she tried to do the same for him, standing over him as he sat at the edge of the bed, he trapped her in the vee of his long thighs, tongued her nipple, then took one in his mouth, and put an end to retreating. She straddled him as he suckled her, and they clung to each other, pushing up their pulse rates until he laid her across the bed and buried himself deep within her. He said her name the same way she'd said his when he'd come to her at the airport. It was all he could manage.

But she said, "Welcome home."

He held her as they lay in bed and allowed her the freedom to touch him wherever she would, which seemed, at the moment, to be her fondest pleasure. It was as though he was the Christmas gift she'd thought unaffordable, and she had to examine every angle for authenticity and then simply touch, again and again, in appreciation. He understood. He had the same need, felt the same pleasure in touching her.

"Miguel said you traded yourself for the others," she said at last. "Is that what you did?"

"Not really. I agreed to stay behind."

"Were you so certain they'd let you go?"

"I was sure at least two out of the three wanted to let all of us go. The odds were in my favor."

She turned her face to his chest and kissed his flat nipple. "I hated coming back without you."

"I hated your being there, Morgan—the better part of me did. But there was a part of me that celebrated because... You're a paradox, you know that? You set aside all your good sense, and you came because I was there.''

"I love you," she told him simply.

He let the words settle in his breast. He knew they were true. He knew, too, that she didn't want them to be. "That's not practical," he said, testing. "I'm a dreamer."

"I know." She sighed, and then repeated, "I know. The worst kind of dreamer. And the best. What you did took a rare kind of courage...and rare talent."

"I couldn't persuade them to let Elizabeth have her baby." His sigh echoed hers. "She made a trade, too, for the others. *That's* rare courage."

"I don't have that kind of courage, Mikal."

He laughed, and his voice rumbled in his chest beneath her ear. "My sensible coward. I couldn't believe my eyes when I saw you there at the palace that first time. Miss Remark! Whatever made you do such a crazy thing?"

"Not knowing made me crazy," she confessed. "Temporarily."

"Temporary insanity?"

"I don't want to be asked to make sacrifices like yours and Elizabeth's. I'm not that noble. I went to that island for purely selfish reasons."

"Love?"

"I'm selfish about the people I love," she said quietly. "I want them with me."

"All the time?"

"Most of the time." She considered, then amended, "At least, *some* of the time. It doesn't matter with dreamers, anyway. Even when they're with you, they're not *really* with you, if you know what I mean."

"No, I don't know what you mean. I have a lot of dreams, Morgan, and lately most of them include..." With two fingers he tilted her chin up as he bent his head to give her a firm kiss. "Am I really with you now?" he demanded.

"Yes." She wouldn't argue. This was the piece of him she knew was hers. She made it hers each time they were together this way.

"Good. If I'm in for an out-of-body experience, I don't want to have it right now." He shifted, cuddling her along his side. He wanted to toy with her hair and admire what he could see of her face in the dim light spilling from the bathroom.

"The boys from the State Department can have exactly one hour tomorrow," he decided. "No more. We're going home for Christmas. Will your father be ready?"

"Tomorrow, yes." She didn't tell him that she'd already made arrangements for going home. She'd made her reservation at the airport shortly before he'd arrived, allowing herself just one more night with him. This was her weakness, she decided, this most beautiful of all dreamers, even though he wasn't for real. Dreamers could never be mistaken for the real thing, for possessors of to-have-and-to-hold-from-this-day-forward dependability. As long as she knew that and recognized that he was, indeed, her weakness, she could afford to give herself one more night. Her weaknesses were few enough, she told herself, and she inhaled deeply of the heady scent belonging to this most cherished one.

"What made them let you go, Mikal?"

"I asked them to," he said, his eyes glistening with pleasure as he watched her hair sift through his fingers. "I told them you were waiting for me."

"No, really, Mikal."

"Okay, really." He tucked her head under his chin and held her close, so she couldn't see his face. "I held them at gunpoint, Morgan. I got the drop on Guerrero and threatened to expose him for the wimp he is if he didn't get me on the next plane out. I held a gun to his head while he drove me to the airport. You should've seen their faces when I sprayed them with my M-16 before I hopped on the plane and ordered the pilot to take off."

Morgan swallowed. "Really? Where was Mc-Quade?"

"He was the tailgunner."

"Tailgunner?"

"We had it all worked out. Plan B. You should've seen me, honey. I was magnificent."

"Tailgunner? You came in on a 747."

His laughter was soundless, but his body shook with it.

"Mikal! Now, *really*."

"*Really*, she keeps saying. You liked the second story so much better than you liked the first, Miss Remark." He kissed the top of her head, then laughed again. "McQuade will love it. My heroic moment."

She squirmed, pulling back to look up at him. "I saw your heroic moment, Mikal, probably one of many. You made Guerrero back down. You made him let my father go. I don't know what you said, because I don't understand Spanish, but I know you got the upper hand somehow, without a gun, without any tailgunner. What did you do?"

"Psyched him out, I guess. I knew you'd risk exposing yourself in order to get medical help for your father, so I had to get him out of there."

"How did *you* get out, then?" she asked again.

He gathered her back in his arms. "I told you," he said. "Castillo's pretty sentimental anyway. I spent a lot of time with him, talked farming, family and poetry, and he agreed to make some diplomatic overtures through me. And I told him—" he traced her jawline with the back of his hand and her collarbone with his thumb "—about my lioness. About the way she nuzzles my neck and purrs. About the way she usually takes a pretty practical position on life in the jungle, but that there are those days—" his hand slid to her breast, and she took a deep breath and filled his palm "—when she arches her back and digs her claws in—" he groaned as she ran her nails lightly along his back and sank them into his buttocks. "And, oh God, can she be a passionate handful then."

\* \* \*

Mikal had an early-morning session with people from the State Department, which he suspected would take more than an hour. Yuri came to the hotel with Alex to pick Mikal up, but then, to Morgan's surprise, he stayed behind. He invited Morgan to have breakfast with him, and she accepted.

After the last cup of coffee was served, Yuri got to the point, for which Morgan had politely waited. She knew he was as practical in his own way as she was in hers and wouldn't have stayed behind without a reason. "I have not married with good reason," he began. "It would interfere with my work. Some men have space in their lives for both. Others don't. If they marry and the work claims them as it is meant to, they feel guilty." He eyed her carefully and with a hint of sympathy. "We don't want that for Mikal, do we?"

"Mikal has been married before," Morgan said evenly. She would not make this easier for Yuri by telling him it was unnecessary. She would make him ply his trade as he endeavored to free Mikal.

Yuri nodded. "And he has a son. Children adjust as the demands become greater. Women like you do not."

"Women like me?"

"You're a woman who can't sit home and wait, can't merely be ready when your man has time for you and be patient when he doesn't. That's the only kind of woman for Mikal now. He's too good at what he does."

"Have you thought about what *Mikal* might want?" she asked.

"You've read his poetry," Yuri reminded her. "You know his vision. He'll give his life for the things he believes in."

Morgan gave the old man a level stare. He was formidable, but she knew who she was. "I have a life, too, Yuri. I have work that I believe in. What's between Mikal and me is our own, and I doubt that you know as much about it as you think you do." She laid her napkin by her cup and stood, enjoying the fact that Yuri looked surprised as he followed suit. "Don't worry. I understand who Mikal Romanov is, and I won't tamper with that."

She was packed and ready to leave when Mikal returned to the hotel at noon. He saw her bags, and she read the confusion in his eyes. "I can't leave until tomorrow," he said, reaching for her. She backed away, and the confusion deepened. "I called David and told him tomorrow for sure. Can you wait another day? We'll go back together."

Morgan shook her head. "I need to get back. My father's ready, and so am I."

Mikal shoved his hands in his pockets and took a step back, giving her space. "Okay. I'll see you at home, then."

"I doubt that my father will stay around Bismarck long," she said quickly. "I want to spend as much time with him as I can, so I probably won't—"

"What's this all about, Morgan?"

In defense, Mikal let his confusion become his quiet form of anger. Morgan decided she could handle that with coolness. "It's not 'about' anything. You have business to take care of here, and I have mine at home. I appreciate all you've done for my father, Mikal."

"For your . . . father?"

Heaving a sigh, she reached abruptly for her suitcase, but when she leaned across the vanity for her purse, Mikal snatched it up first. They stared hotly at one another for several seconds, and then, without glancing away, he took several folded papers from his jacket pocket. He stuffed them into her purse before handing the bag to her and turning to leave.

"Let me know if you're ever free," he told her quietly, and then he closed the door behind him.

Morgan resisted looking at the pages Mikal had given her until her father had fallen asleep next to her on the plane. She opened her purse slowly and peered in, as though she were afraid to touch the papers—as though they might be hot. She felt them gingerly, ran a finger along the thick fold, and finally drew them out. She felt her throat tighten as she unfolded them and found several pages of Mikal's poems, each one dated. This was his book of hours, the difficult ones he'd spent at De Colores. These were the thoughts and fears he'd kept to himself, the frustration and the loneliness. And here was his love for her. He had remembered her and kept himself sane. He had talked to her, praised her, wondered, worried, called her his.

Know me, dark-haired lady
Trust me with your untried passion
Take my constancy to your soft breast
And see the man who loves the paradox in you.

Morgan's hands trembled as she folded the papers carefully and returned them to her purse.

His poetry haunted her. He reached for her with it across time and space, touched her with it, made forgetting him impossible. Dreams, she thought. She couldn't live dreams. She was a practical, down-to-earth woman. But her dreams of him were sweet things—milk and honey—nourishing and earthy. She feasted on remembrances of Mikal's smile, equally charming with his dazzling tux or his favorite sweater, of Mikal's light, easy touch as he prepared a gourmet dish or swept her hair back from her face, and of the sound of Mikal's voice, smooth and commanding in a room teeming with people, or husky and powerful in her ear. There was nothing ethereal about her memories of him. Even as she plunged back into her routine, he was with her, at her shoulder in every move she made. She wasn't sure whether she'd made him part of her reality or become a dreamer herself. Either way, the memories she cherished were of an earthy man whose single fault was that he dreamed. But now, it seemed, Morgan Kramer had learned to dream, too.

\* \* \*

Morgan could smell Mikal's marinara sauce. If she'd had any reservations about ringing the back doorbell, they floated away as the aroma drifted to her nose. Tomatoes and oregano and Mikal's magic. She pressed the button.

The porch light came on, and David peered through the glass. Morgan was glad he opened the door so quickly. It was a still night that had already plummeted deep into the frigid temperatures of a typical Dakota January. He pushed open the storm door and offered an eager, "Miss Kramer! Come on in."

Morgan stepped over the threshold, just avoiding a large pair of running shoes, which David snatched out of her way. "Hey, what a surprise. Dad'll really be— Dad!" he called over one shoulder. To the armload of running shoes, David added a broom and a small collection of newspapers, which he gathered as he backed into the kitchen. "He wasn't expecting you, was he? I mean, it's great you're here in time for supper and all, but . . ." He gave a skinny-shouldered shrug. "We could've picked up a little."

"I'm barging in unannounced because I couldn't resist the smell of that sauce," she told him with a smile. "I don't want to cause any—"

"Hello, Morgan."

The sight of him, the sound of his voice, his very presence, made it hard for her to breathe regularly. "I came to wish you . . . a happy New Year."

He grinned. "The same to you. How's your father?"

"He's fine."

"Spending a lot of time together, are you?"

"Y—yes."

He moved closer, still wearing that grin, this time along with a rust sweater that looked comfortably Mikal. Dazzlingly Mikal. Charmingly Mikal. "Let me take your coat, Morgan. You'll have supper, I hope."

Morgan fumbled with her buttons. "It smells wonderful." When the last button was undone, Morgan raised her head slowly, taking a deep breath, more for courage than enjoyment of the aroma. His blue eyes were soft with understanding. She smiled, quietly adding, "And I *am* free."

Arms piled high with an assortment of misplaced articles, David rounded the corner behind Mikal and disappeared down the hallway. He was back in a moment with his own coat. "Scott just called, Dad. He asked me to stay over tonight, and he's got that new computer. Would you mind?"

"What about supper?"

"We're making pizza. So it's okay? Great seeing you, Miss Kramer. Eat my share." The back door closed on David's last words, "You'll love the marin—"

Mikal was laughing, and Morgan joined in gratefully. "It probably isn't that great seeing me. He just saw me in school today, and I got after him about being tardy."

"How tardy?"

"Not very."

"I guess I have to get after him now, too. About lying."

He'd put her coat over a chair, and now he was looking at her as though she might be the marinara sauce. Her tongue felt awkward as she tried to keep up her end of the conversation. "About what?"

He took her face in his hands and searched her eyes. "Did you hear the phone ring?" She shook her head. "Neither did I. I think he invited himself."

"So did I. You'll have to get after us both."

He smiled. "You first."

Their kiss was a deluge after too long a drought. It washed them over, swirled over hard, dry surfaces, splashed and sluiced, and finally soaked in, drawing them with it, deeply, to soothe aching roots. At last they were able to draw back, to hold and touch and look at one another.

"I love the poems," she whispered. He dipped his chin in acknowledgment. "I brought them back. You probably want to publish them."

"If you love them, they're yours, Morgan. I write poetry for love. Remember?"

"They're beautiful. You should share them."

"I did."

She hugged him close, pillowing her cheek against his sweater. "I see it differently now," she said. "It wasn't something you sought for yourself."

"I wanted to be home," he told her, pressing his hands against her back. "With my son and with you."

"But you'll go again if you have to."

"If I have to," he agreed.

She closed her eyes and breathed deeply of the smell of him. "If you said otherwise, you wouldn't be Mikal. And I love you."

"I'll be around the house and underfoot most of the time, Morgan. And I'm not exactly tidy. You'll be glad when Yuri persuades me to go on a mission, so you can get organized."

"As long as I never have to do any cooking."

He chuckled. "That goes without saying."

She tilted her head back and smiled. "Everything about you is too big for me. Especially your dreams. Are you really Freedom International's heir apparent?"

"Who said that? Yuri?" Morgan nodded. "I'm an idealist, yes, but so are you, lady. You're a teacher, aren't you? I believe in Freedom International, and I'll help out, but I'm a writer by profession. I want to be Steinbeck's heir apparent."

"I've missed you terribly," she confessed.

"It's been hard to stay away. I wanted to go after you and make you love me."

"I've loved you all along." She kissed his chin. "But you're such a dreamer."

"And you say *everything* about me is too big for you?"

"Maybe not *everything*."

One by one, he took the pins from her hair. "I'd say you were due for a little awareness rally."

Pressing herself closer, she soon made him groan with delight. "For your sake, we'd better make this a private rally. One thing about your awareness, Mikal Romanov—" she slipped her thumbs inside the waistband at the back of his jeans "—it's easily raised."

Mikal laughed as Morgan stood on tiptoe, angling for another kiss. He lifted her in his arms, and Morgan Kramer found joy in what once would have felt like a precarious position—her feet dangling above the floor and her head in the clouds.

\* \* \* \* \*

# READERS' COMMENTS ON SILHOUETTE SPECIAL EDITIONS:

"I just finished reading the first six Silhouette Special Edition Books and I had to take the opportunity to write you and tell you how much I enjoyed them. I enjoyed all the authors in this series. Best wishes on your Silhouette Special Editions line and many thanks."

—B.H.*, Jackson, OH

"The Special Editions are really special and I enjoyed them very much! I am looking forward to next month's books."

—R.M.W.*, Melbourne, FL

"I've just finished reading four of your first six Special Editions and I enjoyed them very much. I like the more sensual detail and longer stories. I will look forward each month to your new Special Editions."

—L.S.*, Visalia, CA

"Silhouette Special Editions are — 1.) Superb! 2.) Great! 3.) Delicious! 4.) Fantastic! . . . Did I leave anything out? These are books that an adult woman can read . . . I love them!"

—H.C.*, Monterey Park, CA

*names available on request

# Take 4 Silhouette Desire novels
## and a surprise gift
## ❧ FREE ❧

Then preview 6 brand-new Silhouette Desire novels—delivered to your door as soon as they come off the presses! If you decide to keep them, you pay just $2.24 each*—a 10% saving off the retail price, *with no additional charges for postage and handling!*

Silhouette Desire novels are not for everyone. They are written especially for the woman who wants a more satisfying, more deeply involving reading experience. Silhouette Desire novels take you beyond the others.

Start with 4 Silhouette Desire novels and a surprise gift absolutely FREE. They're yours to keep without obligation. You can always return a shipment and cancel at any time.

Simply fill out and return the coupon today!

* Plus 69¢ postage and handling per shipment in Canada.

# ATTRACTIVE, SPACE SAVING BOOK RACK

Display your most prized novels on this handsome and sturdy book rack. The hand-rubbed walnut finish will blend into your library decor with quiet elegance, providing a practical organizer for your favorite hard-or soft-covered books.

**Only $9.95**

*Approximately 16" x 8" when assembled*

*Assembles in seconds!*

------------------------------------------------

To order, rush your name, address and zip code, along with a check or money order for $10.70* ($9.95 plus 75¢ postage and handling) payable to *Silhouette Books.*

Silhouette Books
Book Rack Offer
901 Fuhrmann Blvd.
P.O. Box 1396
Buffalo, NY 14269-1396

*Offer not available in Canada.*

BKR-2A

*New York and Iowa residents add appropriate sales tax.

## Silhouette Intimate Moments

# NEXT MONTH
# CHECK IN TO
# DODD MEMORIAL HOSPITAL!

Not feeling sick, you say? That's all right, because Dodd Memorial isn't your average hospital. At Dodd Memorial you don't need to be a patient—or even a doctor yourself!—to examine the private lives of the doctors and nurses who spend as much time healing broken hearts as they do healing broken bones.

In UNDER SUSPICION (Intimate Moments #229) intern Allison Schuyler and Chief Resident Cruz Gallego strike sparks from the moment they meet, but they end up with a lot more than love on their minds when someone starts stealing drugs—and Allison becomes the main suspect.

In May look for AFTER MIDNIGHT (Intimate Moments #237) and finish the trilogy in July with HEARTBEATS (Intimate Moments #245).

Author Lucy Hamilton is a former medical librarian whose husband is a doctor. Let her check you in to Dodd Memorial—you won't want to check out!

# *Silhouette Romance*™
# *Legendary Lovers Trilogy*

## BY DEBBIE MACOMBER....

**ONCE UPON A TIME**, in a land not so far away, there lived a girl, Debbie Macomber, who grew up dreaming of castles, white knights and princes on fiery steeds. Her family was an ordinary one with a mother and father and one wicked brother, who sold copies of her diary to all the boys in her junior high class.

One day, when Debbie was only nineteen, a handsome electrician drove by in a shiny black convertible. Now Debbie knew a prince when she saw one, and before long they lived in a two-bedroom cottage surrounded by a white picket fence.

As often happens when a damsel fair meets her prince charming, children followed, and soon the two-bedroom cottage became a four-bedroom castle. The kingdom flourished and prospered, and between soccer games and car pools, ballet classes and clarinet lessons, Debbie thought about love and enchantment and the magic of romance.

One day Debbie said, "What this country needs is a good fairy tale." She remembered how well her diary had sold and she dreamed again of castles, white knights and princes on fiery steeds. And so the stories of Cinderella, Beauty and the Beast, and Snow White were reborn....

---

**Look for Debbie Macomber's *Legendary Lovers* trilogy from Silhouette Romance: *Cindy and the Prince* (January, 1988); *Some Kind of Wonderful* (March, 1988); *Almost Paradise* (May, 1988). Don't miss them!**

SRT-1